Miss Budge In Love

The Short Adventures
of Mildred Budge

by Daphne Simpkins

Contents

Foreword. 5

1. Getting Real with Men Folk. 7
2. Miss Budge in Love 15
3. Every Hair on Your Head is Numbered 19
4. The Aura of Love 25
5. Follow the Bouncing Ball. 33
6. Miss Budge Chooses a Fearless Life 37
7. Commitment Sunday. 43
8. Christmas Right Now 47
9. The Martha Problem 53
10. Backslid Christian. 57
11. Fasting on the Fifth Sunday of the Month . . 63
12. Onward Christian Soldiers. 71
13. Turkey Dog 79
14. A Christmas Treat. 87

15. Beating a Message of Retreat. 95

16. Naptime on the Prayer Chain 105

17. I've Got Your Number 113

18. Loading an Imprecatory Prayer. 119

19. Vows and Codicils. 125

20. Cleaning House 131

21. Miss Budge Sows a Wild Oat (or Not). 137

22. Lessons In Picking Up a Man At Church . . 141

23. The Artist and Mildred Budge. 147

Acknowledgments 163

Foreword

Miss Budge In Love: The Short Adventures of Mildred Budge is a collection of short stories about friendship within a church and the kind of faith-driven questions that many people naturally wrestle with every day. Many of them have been published in *The Christian Courier* and *Esprit* in Canada but also in the United States in *Evangel* and on *Churchmousepublications.com* . I am grateful to the editors of these and other periodicals who have understood that people of faith enjoy the kind of adventures that Mildred Budge and her friends have—adventures born in friendship.

I have found friendship in the company of women in my Berean Sunday school class. And readers may find snippets of conversation or events inside these pages that emerged from a real moment in time with my friends, but those authentic catalysts of inspiration from real life have produced what is now truly fiction. No person should be held accountable for any offense or interpretation that these stories might engender, other than myself. However, if there is anything to praise in the characters of these stories, admire the women whose lives touched mine and, in part, inspired the creation of Mildred Budge and her friends. This collection is in their honor:

Carol Henry
Fran Howland
Betty Little
Guin Nance
Anne Henry Tidmore

Getting Real
With Men Folk

"I don't think he really meant to pat me on the fanny. I think he's short and that's where his hand landed," Mildred Budge explained to her best friend Fran.

"Get real, sister," Fran said, taking hold of an expression that their friend Marjorie had introduced at the last Lunch Bunch meeting, when she explained how she survived her ordeal at the hospital after a heart attack ("I said to myself, 'Get real, Marjorie, or you won't walk out of here.'"). Marjorie had walked out with the power of getting real energizing her. Her friends respected this mantra and had been taking "get real" surveys of themselves since then.

"You are not that tall, Mildred Budge, and the man who patted your fanny was not that short. Get real," Fran repeated, smacking her lips. She liked the expression quite a lot.

"Well, he was German, and maybe in Germany men pat women on the fannies in what is considered respectful admiration," Mildred replied ruminatively. She would have let the fanny-patting incident go undiscussed if it had not been observed. But Fran had seen it happen at the reception after a concert and had since then had a lot to say about it. While Mildred valued the counsel of her best friend, sometimes it was easier to get real alone.

"What universe do you live in?" Fran asked, standing still. A pose of stillness was unusual for Fran, who was known far and wide as a mover and a shaker.

"I live in this universe, but I have never understood men very well. You know that," Mildred replied peacefully.

"The problem you have with men is that you think they are deep and mysterious, but they aren't so mysterious. Sure, they don't discuss feelings as easily—generally speaking—and they don't like to come to Sunday school as naturally as some women—generally speaking—which is why we have a special class of husbands who have been prayed into a Sunday school by their wives; and a man—generally speaking—might knock on a bathroom door loudly, even though he knows you're in there when you've asked him for all of your entire married life not to try and speak to you when you're in the bathroom. But, after you have become acquainted with these little, little differences, you would rightly know, Mildred Budge, that no man would pat a woman he doesn't know very well on her *petrushka*."

Part of Fran's mover-and-shaker reputation was built on her innate ability to spontaneously invent words that sounded like what she meant. Mildred thought Fran's invention for *hiney* sounded more Russian than German; but in the culture of the American Deep South, where strong consonants and elongated vowel sounds move easily from speech to song and helped invent the music that originated there—the Blues—Mildred understood that Fran was talking about any behind, of any nationality.

As if reading her mind, Fran shook her head, made that tsk-tsk-tsking sound she clucked when she felt sorry for how naïve her friend Mildred was, and said, "Well, the German was not in love with you, Mildred. You do know that, don't you?"

Mildred nodded, of course. She had never thought he was. She would not have thought much about the pat if Fran had not seen it happen and kept bringing it up.

"I suspect, Millie—and I'm sorry that I have to be the one to tell you this—that he simply saw your belvedere, liked the shape of it, and gave it a pat. You've been walking a lot, and your belvedere has tightened up."

Mildred's newly tightened derriere had been undeniably transformed by a rigorous walking program that had, in an age when miracles were supposed to be over, reduced her clothing size. In the course of her dedicated morning walks, she had found herself, upon rare occasions, possibly running, too. Mildred did not report that she was jogging, because she wasn't sure she was. For most of her life, she had been known as a notoriously slow walker, and it was possible that she was only walking faster than she ever had before and that increased tempo now felt, to her, like running.

She was curious about the truth—wanted to get real. There were a couple of times during these brief bursts of what felt like speed on her morning walk that she wanted to ask another exerciser as she passed her by, "Am I running or still only walking?" But even she knew that others would not be able to process that question and answer it without becoming suspicious of her mental capability and then might try to lock her up in the institution that Marjorie had successfully escaped. Getting real was harder than one might suppose.

"You were a temptation, Mildred. And the German succumbed to it. Does that help you to understand this matter of the flesh?" Fran pressed.

It had been a long time since Mildred had thought of herself as a temptation to anyone. Rather, she had reached an age where she more often heard that she reminded people of their mothers. They usually wanted advice or a recipe, and it was usually the kind of advice she seemed to have or a recipe that she could easily find.

And then, that nice German man had sat beside her at the concert and, later at the reception, had told her stories of his travels, and she had been enraptured with all of the places he had been. Even though she had to look down to make eye contact with him, Mildred had not been uncomfortable, not like she usually was in some close quarters with other men, particularly men in the church who had been trained by every pastor whose likeness was hung in the series of portraits on the parlor wall at church to never be alone with a woman, and if you are, make sure the door is open and stay on your feet. Avoid even the appearance of evil!

There was something to be said about discretion between the sexes, but also a time (though there was nothing about it in Ecclesiastes) to be together fearlessly—not so much fearless of sin but not afraid of what you will do. Getting real with herself, Mildred Budge was not afraid of what she might do under any circumstances, and she had not been afraid of the implications of the fanny pat, either when it happened or since Fran had dissected it.

In Fran's presence—and because she respected Marjorie's emphatic recommendation that everyone should get real about their daily lives—Mildred's mind roamed around words under which to file the fanny-patting incident. She thought of temptation, sin, impropriety, and then the truest word that catalogued her own response: affection.

The German's pat had been a quick, friendly move, she thought, more like a fond wave of farewell that had landed on her *belvedere*. There was no insult intended, she thought; and she had not taken any.

She would have told Fran that, but she understood that Fran believed that any lady—any got-real Christian lady—should have been indignant over such an outrage.

But Mildred was not indignant. Not outraged. She just felt the warm, genial glow of the German's eyes. At the end of their conversation and, because they would never see one another again, they had shared a clumsy *ta-ta* embrace; and as they parted, his hand had slipped off her waist, and finding itself in a strange place, had patted her twice—bye-bye—and then his hand withdrew, while his eyes continued to smile, as if to say, "*Pardon me. I meant no disrespect.*"

She had walked away smiling, with her dignity intact, smiling more than a church lady usually did, for she had not only been seen and heard and talked with, but touched companionably, like an old friend.

Like players do on the football field.

Like guys on the basketball court.

Like baseball players who are called "safe" by the umpire.

Like that.

Yes, like that.

She wanted to tell Fran that—that not all touching is axiomatically sin—that there can be something safe that adds something bright like a candle's glow to unexpected moments, but Fran wasn't finished. "Do you remember how that guy tried to get you to go for a ride on his motorcycle and you thought he was asking you for directions? I had to explain that to you, too."

Mildred had forgotten about the man on the motorcycle, but when she remembered the tattooed man with the long, flowing, red hair and the toothy smile, she could not stifle the smile that came with the remembered surprise, when he had zoomed up beside her in front of the drug store and asked her if she wanted to hop on and ride to Birmingham. "I don't know the way to Birmingham," Mildred had said. She did know, actually, but she couldn't remember which way to go in that moment of being surprised.

"You'd be married today if you just lived in the same universe with the rest of us. But you don't," Fran declared. "But that's okay. I'll keep explaining how it all works to you, until you understand."

Getting real, Mildred doubted that. Doubted that everything that happened between men and women all the time could be understood and filed away in a perfect category. When she thought about some of her warmest memories, none of them seemed to fit a place where in the explaining—of getting real—someone else could understand what "it" had meant to her.

"What are you thinking about, Mildred Budge? Have you told me everything?" Fran asked.

Mildred offered her a mysterious imitation of the Giaconda smile, and Fran shook her head, wagged a finger, and warned, "You better get real, Mildred Budge, because for the record, you are so not a biker chick."

Miss Budge in Love

Mildred Budge was sitting in the balcony of the Davis Theatre in downtown Montgomery, watching Debbie Reynolds perform, when the lady beside her complained, "My hiney has gone to sleep."

"My foot has," Miss Budge replied companionably.

"But doesn't Debbie Reynolds look good?" the woman added.

Miss Budge nodded. Debbie Reynolds did sparkle in a blue sheath dress, and she still sang with all of the gusto of the unsinkable Molly Brown.

Mildred Budge hummed along as Miss Reynolds crooned her signature hit that closed the special evening concert, "Tammy's in Love."

Dull eyes sparkled even more then. Cold hearts, already warmed by the nostalgia of Miss Reynolds' career retold in music, grew warmer still. Then, as people applauded and stood up, Mildred Budge rose and began the awkward task of clambering over the chubby knees of the lady with the hibernating hiney, who said, "I can't move yet. You go on."

It wasn't easy. Mildred's left foot was still asleep, and her best navy church-going skirt was tighter tonight than ever before. Growing older was hard, but gaining weight was easy.

Miss Budge had just found her footing in the center aisle, when a nearby gentleman suddenly hit the carpeted floor face-first. Miss Budge crossed immediately to his side and knelt down. His skin was clammy, his breathing raspy. Cradling the man's head against her ample bosom, she spoke as if she were still a schoolteacher whose job was to call the class to order. "Someone call an ambulance, please."

When she spoke, the man's gray eyes popped open.

Oh, how the man's scared gaze triggered memories for Miss Budge, of taking care of her daddy when he had been terminally ill. This dear fellow wore the same type of white cotton shirt her daddy had liked and which she had always laundered specially. His Old Spice cologne was rife in the air, for the poor man had broken out into a flop sweat that signaled a serious inner discord.

"Don't try to get up just yet," Mildred said, as his eyes flickered, searching for more help—for meaning. *What was happening to him?*

The gentleman did not know that he had fallen into the arms of a church lady, whose whole nature and body had been waking up to new unctions to pray, with more and more of her whole self all the time.

On Miss Budge's morning constitutionals, she often fought the urge to fall to her knees on warming asphalt to pray for people driving to work and for teenagers going to school. And at home, when the phone rang with a prayer-chain request, Miss Budge usually collapsed to her knees before she could hang up the phone.

But in that moment, Miss Budge wanted to offer her body as a healing place for the man with the scared gray eyes. Instantly, prayers from her inner Miss Budge left her soul like spontaneously created love songs—composed not only for the man but also for all the people Miss Budge had ever loved.

Prayer was like that. The experiences of a lifetime often came together to create the prayer of the moment for someone in need.

And, as the prayers left her in groans too deep for spoken words, Miss Budge crooned to the man, "It's all right. You'll be all right."

The sweating eased. His fear diminished. He blinked. Smiled self-consciously. And then he sat up.

As the sound of a siren approached, the crowd murmured, "The poor fellow must have fainted. That's all. What's with that crazy woman who won't let go of him?"

A stranger clucked behind her, "Old women will be the death of us all."

Someone finally took a solid grip on Mildred's elbows and hoisted her up to her feet. She stepped back while others moved in to ask his name—he knew it—and where he lived—he said it—and who was with him. "I'm alone," he said.

The announcement of his aloneness startled people, but Mildred Budge knew the truth: he wasn't alone.

No one was alone, but there were still too many people who didn't know that the God of creation was waiting for them, crooning to them, calling out in love, "Come to me and be healed—find rest."

She looked around. The field was ripe for harvest, and Miss Budge breathed her "Save them, Jesus" prayer that was like a love song that played inside of her all the time. Miss Budge had been in love with God for most of her life. Like Debbie Reynolds, she had a lot of music in her. Miss Budge hummed more of her "Rescue the perishing, Jesus" prayer as she slipped out the back door and made her way to the street.

Outside, the evening was cool and starlit, the air fragrant with magnolia and honeysuckle. The concrete sidewalk pulsed with stored sunshine, and Miss Budge stopped for a moment to absorb with gratitude the sweetness of being alive and to watch as the paramedics went inside and then came out alone.

"Thank you, Jesus," she said automatically.

Other concert-goers passed her by, barely seeing her in the dark, except to notice that she was another one of those older women who always seemed to be talking to herself and fidgeting for keys while wondering where it was exactly that she had parked her car.

Every Hair on Your Head is Numbered

It bothered Mildred Budge that the governor's wife did not comb the back of her hair properly.

Every time the woman came on TV, the camera caught the First Lady from the back, and her teased brown hair looked like a tumbleweed.

Maybe the style was intentional. Messy hair seemed to be the norm now. Maybe messy hair wasn't really messy, if it was considered a proper hairstyle.

Mildred sighed, sending the question to that place in her brain where she stored recurrent ruminations that preoccupied her when insomnia hit—or maybe caused it.

Today, she had a different question to answer. The retired schoolteacher was determined to sit outside and practice the Presence of God, a spiritual discipline that cropped up periodically in her quiet-time reading.

The writer she was currently reading made a distinction between ways of practicing God's Presence: meditation was a focus; contemplation was being open to whatever came.

As Miss Budge settled onto the blue chaise lounge on her back porch, she decided that she was going to contemplate—and almost immediately she remembered the governor's wife's messy hair. Her hand involuntarily reached for an imagined comb and found the metal arms of the chaise lounge. The hot metal reminded Miss Budge where she was. She resolved to focus and recited the writer's suggested first step in learning to contemplate.

1. Collect your desire for God.

Understanding desire had always been hard for Mildred, because she had always been mostly content.

Mildred stroked the back of her head thoughtfully. Something felt wrong. Her hair felt thin back there. Instantly, Mildred remembered how her hairdresser had gently, and without any discussion, begun separating a significant portion of Miss Budge's bangs to grow over one side of Mildred's head.

Mildred bolted upright. *I have a comb-over!* Mildred realized suddenly. She was stricken. Even as she had been assessing the governor's wife's ill-kempt hairdo, she might have a worse problem of her own: blinding vanity.

The speck/plank issue often gave Mildred Budge starts of realization that led to repentance. "Sorry," she said to God, as she checked her watch. She had been practicing the Presence for two minutes—eight minutes to go.

Contemplation was hard.

Determined to come back to step one later, she moved on to step two.

2. Listen to your inner voice and find your heart's prayer.

Mildred tilted her head to listen to her inner voice, and it said, "You may be losing your hair."

She automatically recited a few of the many disciplined answers that she knew to use when fear attacked: "Everything is vanity. Dust to dust. Thy will be done."

Then, she remembered something her hairdresser Michael had often said to her and the other ladies: "Darling, it's only hair."

She smiled when she thought of Michael and how, when she first sat down in his chair, he held her gaze in the mirror. That mattered. Deeply. For when a woman sat down in her beautician's chair, she was suddenly confronted with a hard look at herself. She always chose to meet Michael's gaze in the glass instead. Michael always saw her with affection, his brown eyes beaming in welcome. What a gift his gaze was—more important to Miss Budge, really, than the way his hands and scissors moved about her head. Miss Budge loved Michael. All the ladies did.

A welcome breeze stirred the gardenia bush then, and a fragrant white petal wafted and then landed in Miss Budge's ample lap. Her hand instinctively reached for the tender flower. She paused to enjoy its fragility— was preparing to contemplate its beauty and then meditate on it—but grew almost immediately solemn when she saw yet another of her precious brown hairs stuck to it.

"God have mercy," she prayed automatically.

No wonder so many of her girlfriends at church were worried: thinning hair was a universal concern. The inevitable Biblical truth wafted to her consciousness as gracefully as a flower's petal: "Every hair on your head is numbered."

Holding the petal, she mused, "God counts the falling sparrows, but don't they all fall? People, too?"

Mildred sighed. Six minutes to go. The sun was too hot. The blue net weaving felt scratchy against her legs. She felt fat. Maybe Michael could work her in later that afternoon. He knew the names of volumizing shampoos.

Miss Budge decided then to postpone her experiment in contemplation and devote the remaining minutes of her prayer time to intercessory prayer instead.

She began by praying for the governor's wife; bless her heart. Then, Miss Budge prayed for all of her friends and their problems. She prayed for Michael, and smiled. Michael's steadfast acceptance reminded Mildred that Jesus looked at her with love, too—only better. She breathed some of Jesus' promises: "Cast your cares upon me. Come unto me and I will give you rest. I go to prepare a place for you. If it were not so, I would have told you." Miss Budge believed everything Jesus said and trusted Him about what He didn't explain.

Burdens lifted then. She started talking. "Thank you, Jesus, for life and for all that you are all the time, whether I understand you or not," Miss Budge said. Then she pushed herself up.

Standing, Mildred Budge knew that she had not fulfilled her mission—found a definitive heart's prayer that fit the order of contemplation from a book she admired. But her soul felt lighter and her heart, which just minutes before had been fraught with anxieties, had found a radiant stillness inside that caused her not to worry about hairstyles or new ways to pray or even what would seem in about fifteen minutes another profoundly important question: what would she have for lunch?

The Aura of Love

Mildred Budge walked through the door of the new hair salon she was forced to try, because her regular beauty consultant, stylist, and yes, at times, her confessor, had been summoned by an actress to keep her locks tended while on location in Miss Budge's home state of Alabama.

The loss of Michael had left a hole Miss Budge could not fill. Nor could she find a replacement. She had waited a long time for Michael simply to come back to her, and now, with hair too long to manage, Mildred had decided to try this other lady, Zenia, a Hair Master who not only styled hair but also conducted yoga workshops in between hair appointments.

There was a strange sign on the front door of Zenia's Salon that listed all of the services that men and women could buy once they crossed the magic threshold of beauty, and Miss Budge recognized most of them; but the last one, written in a child's hand and slanted, not in a line, but sort of uphill, perplexed her. "Ear candling."

Inside, the receptionist translated the expression on Miss Budge's face and explained, "Ear candling is new here, and it's just the thing. Everybody's doing it."

A chorus of people emerged out of nowhere, like they do at restaurants when a customer's birthday is revealed, a cupcake is produced, and the celebratory song is sung. Only this time, the chorus chanted praise for ear candling: "You must have it done at least twice a year. At least! You will be shocked at what comes out of your ears."

By then, Zenia the Hair Master emerged from the small hallway where she had a chair with a mirror in front of it. Taking Miss Budge by the elbow, this woman who was not Michael steered Miss Budge toward what wasn't quite a room. It was more like a hallway with a chair. People came and went through it while a patron got snipped and fluffed.

Carefully and unaided, Miss Budge climbed up onto the raised black chair. It was in that moment that she truly missed her Michael, for he had always instinctively understood that a lady did not always want to see so much of herself so quickly in a very big mirror. Michael had a way of touching her shoulder as she ascended onto the beauty chair—the way a doctor does reassuringly, just before he gives you a tetanus shot. Then, when Michael helped a woman look into a mirror—and he believed in facing the truth, albeit kindly—dear Michael's clientele didn't see someone for whom the blush was off the rose but a woman with a handsome man standing beside her, smiling, who didn't just see clearly how you did look but who had an affectionate vision for how you did look and could look.

In that moment, Miss Budge stared into Zenia's mirror and blinked back tears. Involuntarily, she whispered to the place where her previous hairdresser should have been standing, "Michael. Michael. Michael."

Sitting in a strange hairdresser's chair, Miss Budge felt unfaithful to Michael and abandoned by him all at the same time. She squeezed her eyes closed, until the plastic sheet was wrapped around her. When she opened them, she was still alone and now disappointed, because the cape was one of those severe black and white animal prints. Why couldn't it just be pink or even brown? Miss Budge looked her best in brown.

"Ear candling is therapeutic. I do it for all of my family members," Zenia confided. "Shall we make it a day of beauty?" she then asked, her nose wrinkling like a rabbit's.

"Could you follow the haircut I have? Michael designed it just for me. He was—is—a hair-styling genius," Mildred replied.

Zenia's eyes registered a flash of anger at the mention of Michael the genius, as if her creativity was being hampered because her predecessor had been talented in his work. Miss Budge took a deep breath and asked God to help her go with the flow, to become a people person, to be thankful in all circumstances. Seated in a stranger's beauty chair, she prayed for Michael's safety and fulfillment in his work, and, yes, she tried to purpose in her heart to pray for That Movie Star— that Other Woman with more money than all of his long-time customers put together—who had seduced, seduced, seduced Michael away from all of the women who were devoted to him. The bitterness of being left was irrationally reinterpreted as being scorned, a brief glint of pain that zigged and zagged through Miss Budge's memories, touching on all of the times when Miss Budge, a retired public school teacher who had become a full-time church lady, had been thwarted in love.

And while Miss Budge's mind darted, Zenia's scissors snipped here and there, sometimes touching her hair, sometimes not. "I am finding the aura of Meez Budge's head in order to release youth and health," Zenia explained as she snipped into outer space. "Your aura eez so dim," Zenia said disapprovingly.

Once a doctor's nurse had told size-14 Miss Budge that she was technically obese, and Miss Budge, not knowing exactly what to say when a stranger tells you you're fat, had replied, thinly, "Thank you."

Miss Budge said those words again, this time to Zenia.

"I could move you on over to ear candling in the next room. They have an opening, if you'd like to clear your thoughts," Zenia suggested, whipping the cloth away violently, like a bullfighter.

"That's what ear candling does?" Miss Budge asked, climbing down from the chair without looking at her haircut. It didn't matter how it looked. Her aura was dim. It was old, like her. Michael had gone off with another woman. She was going to die one day. Life was sad.

Zenia picked up a slender candle and held it out to Miss Budge. "See haw tha candle iz empty in the middle?" Zenia's accent faded, and she began to speak with a drawl that was indigenous to Slapout, Alabama. "Stick it in an ear, and light it. Dang, if the heat doesn't work like a chimney does, drawing stuff up and out of yore big old ear. We got a fingernail out of an ear one time. A false fingernail!" Zenia spoke the words with emphasis, as if it were a better thing to get a false fingernail out of an ear than a real one.

Miss Budge looked through the inside of the bored-out candle, and her aura shifted. Her mind returned. Michael seemed a long way off, and she was going to have to soldier on. Her shoulders went back as she looked up at Zenia. "I don't think it would do my eardrums any good if a drop of hot wax landed inside my ear canal."

Zenia processed that idea, her dark eyes narrowing, as she laid aside the candle and decided to charge the older woman double, so she wouldn't come back bringing her tiresome aura with her. Unhip women were simply too much trouble. Everyone said so, and they didn't tip good, neither. The only reason Zenia had taken this one was that Miss Budge promised that she didn't want her hair rolled or dried. Who rolled their hair anymore?

Miss Budge placed her hairdresser's tip discreetly on the table and walked back to the register to settle her exorbitant bill, not surprised by the high price or confused by what it ultimately meant. Before getting in her car, Miss Budge faced the idea that she would have to find yet another hairdresser, for she understood what being overcharged meant. And she wondered how her Michael was doing, and if he was so far away that she couldn't drive to wherever he was. Would he mind? Would he be glad to see her? Would he have to pretend? Had he always pretended the way a salesman did with customers? The idea saddened her more than anything Zenia had said. Miss Budge tried to remember Michael's eyes.

Already, she almost couldn't.

It would be six weeks before she would need to solve the problem of a haircut again, and while she was too old to have her ears candled, Miss Budge was old enough to know how to wait and hope.

She got into her red and black MINI Cooper and intended to drive the long way home, though she had an urge to take the bridge to the small town nearby. Sometimes, Miss Budge liked to drive over that bridge because, once upon a time, she had gone home that way on the Fourth of July, and picnicking people had launched fireworks from the river's bank. She had pulled over to the side of the bridge and watched the fireworks light up the late evening sky and thought of all the times that movie directors had used that special effect to signal passion happening between lovers. Miss Budge could almost remember how fireworks looked over the Alabama River.

She headed to the bridge, looking down at the water into which jilted lovers had occasionally thrown themselves but rarely died. In the South, brokenhearted lovers could usually swim, despite their intentions, when they threw themselves off the bridge. The stories often made the newspapers, and the romance of romance became the stuff of Southern folklore.

She passed over the bridge, the river. The memory of fireworks and the sight of the water gave her an idea. She steered her car into the nearest drugstore's parking lot. Telling herself brightly that she was really just popping in for a can of hairspray, Miss Budge found herself looking at the scissors that were sold on the hair products aisle. She bought a pair.

For in that post-Michael, post-Zenia moment, Miss Budge couldn't face looking for another hairdresser. She would not even try. With a good pair of scissors, she would not have to brace herself for more high chairs that were hard to climb onto and deal with dark patterned capes that made her look corpselike—auraless and dim.

She batted back a surprising tear. Looking ahead, Miss Budge already knew that if Michael didn't return from that man-stealing movie star, she would go to the river on a day when no one was going to jump or set off fireworks. There, where women had mourned the loss of love in dramatic ways, she would take out her scissors and cut off her hair and toss it by the handful into the gently coursing Alabama River.

"And that is how I will wear it until Michael returns— or until I die," she pledged, as she got back inside her car. She placed the scissors reverently into her glove compartment next to her car maintenance schedule, her insurance proof, her emergency ten dollar bill, and a postage stamp.

* * *

Months later, after she had found another hair dresser who was not Zenia, Miss Budge was buying gas and needed that ten dollar bill. She opened her glove compartment and was instantly reassured by the sight of the maintenance schedule, which her mechanic dutifully marked, and her registration that no policeman had ever asked to see, and felt wasteful about the emergency postage stamp that had begun to curl up in the heat and most likely would no longer stick to any envelope—and now needed a 3-cent booster stamp to make it fly. Did they sell 3-cent stamps? Before the answer came, Miss Budge saw the pair of new scissors and was puzzled.

As faithful women through the centuries have done, who have loved deeply and stumbled upon a souvenir of a previous potent relationship, the scissors triggered a faint memory but no real reference to any specific occasion. Something deep inside her right ear begin to itch, and Miss Budge said ruminatively, "What are these scissors doing in here?"

Follow the Bouncing Ball

When Mildred heard the TV morning show guest report that therapists often play a game of catch with male patients to establish rapport, she leaned closer to the screen.

"Because men often interpret conversation as a form of aggression," the male therapist said, visibly stiffening as the perky TV hostess leaned closer and smiled encouragingly for the man to continue talking. "That's why they sit sideways," the man said, looking at her sideways. "On guard against attack."

Are they on guard? Does conversation feel like that to men? Mildred wondered.

Did the answer have relevance?

Mildred was a single woman of a seasoned age, and though she had certainly turned down proposals (it was easy when a man asked over a hot dog, "Why don't me and you get married?"), she often had problems communicating clearly with men and had never understood why.

At times, she blamed her antiquated vocabulary. Just thinking about the word *antiquated* impelled Mildred to say out loud, "Groovy," a word that had gone to sleep for a while and woken back up, as the really good words should and sometimes do.

But this business of a bouncing ball being employed ingeniously to make a connection with men, well, it felt inspired to her. And so the next time she passed a vending machine at the grocery store that sold a bouncing ball for a quarter, Mildred Budge invested fifty cents and bought two potential conversational ice breakers.

Buying a second ball quickly proved to be a groovy idea, for as soon as Miss Budge attempted to dribble the one with blue and white swirls, it got away from her and rolled off down the street. She prudently placed the other one—a black and white miniature soccer ball— in her purse, next to her spare set of house keys, for the likely looking potential conversational partner and opportune moment when she could test this new idea of playing ball with a man in order to have a real conversation.

Initially, no stranger on the street looked groovy enough, though there was a man coming out of the gas station who held the door for her and very chirpily said to her rear end as she passed through, "There you go, pretty lady."

"Thank you, handsome stranger," Mildred replied, as her hand inched toward the bouncing ball. No time to follow through, however. The man didn't hear her, for a diesel- burning truck steered loudly away from the pump right at that moment and drowned out the potential rapport that might have developed from the serendipitous encounter.

The next time Miss Budge felt tempted to use the ball as an ice breaker was during the morning worship service when the deacon who made the announcements—not the preacher—stood up and whispered the news of the week in monosyllables, imparting very little information to inquiring Christian minds that wanted to know the details of who had been born, how much the newborn weighed, who had died, and when the funeral was.

Mildred would have asked the whispering deacon to speak up, but calling out from a pew was considered rude in her church. Only, when the person who was supposed to speak has some real information but can't be heard, she found herself provoked to do something about it. She was stirred to reach for the remaining miniature black and white soccer ball in her purse.

She was halfway thinking about sending it dribbling down the aisle to catch the deacon's attention, when she realized that there was a small boy on his knees in the next pew staring at her sideways. The little fellow espied Miss Budge's miniature soccer ball, and his eyes lit up, as if he wanted to say something.

Mildred, the prepared churchwoman who routinely pulled from her purse Advil, Kleenex, and cough drops for whoever was sitting nearby and needed any of them, automatically handed the ball to the young man. Trained to be polite by his mother, grandmother, aunt, sister, and the wives of deacons and elders who were his Sunday school teachers, the little boy leaned forward and opened his mouth to speak, to say thank you, but Miss Budge automatically raised one finger to her lips and whispered incongruously what might be one of the causes of problems that inhibit communication between men and women throughout their lives, "Shsssssssh."

Miss Budge Chooses
a Fearless Life

Mildred Budge was just walking into her favorite store when a man clutching a woman's purse dashed by her. A pretty housewife in white tennis clothes chased the purse snatcher, screaming, "Thief! Thief!"

Automatically, Mildred Budge clutched her own purse tighter and prayed, "Lord, save us from ourselves."

As the running man bounded into an old pickup truck, the lady jumped onto his back bumper, still screaming, "Thief! Thief!"

The man tossed the stolen handbag out the window. The housewife leapt from the truck and went to reclaim her treasure.

"That was a dangerous thing to do," Miss Budge told God, for in her daily life there were not many other people to tell the story of her life to. In this way, Miss Budge engaged in what is known as unceasing prayer. Then, feeling inexplicably wounded by witnessing a thief in action and a woman putting herself in harm's way for what would surely rust this side of heaven, Miss Budge walked inside and over to the store's snack bar.

Miss Budge was not hungry, but her stomach felt troubled by the image of a thief stealing a woman's purse, and because right after she prayed, she had looked down at the items on her shopping list and suddenly didn't want them. Confronting that loss of appetite was frightening.

Feeling pale, she ordered French fries and a chocolate shake. Miss Budge drank several deep swallows. It tasted cheap and artificial, but it was cold and anesthetizing. She drank some more to get her money's worth. Miss Budge had gained weight over the years just getting her money's worth out of cheap-tasting food. The French fries were hot and salty, though. Mildred Budge loved salt and sugar—often together, though neither one of them was good for one's health. As she considered this paradox in her own behavior, she saw the woman whose purse had been stolen reappear in the doorway. Talking animatedly with the store guard, the victim suddenly pointed at Miss Budge and said, "That lady saw it all!"

The officer walked purposefully over to Mildred, who now felt faint. The strangest waves of weakness were washing over her, and she wondered if the Evil One was attacking her; he did that sometimes. But Miss Budge had never been sure of when the Evil One was the true villain or when her own nature reflected the effects of the Fall, which people didn't discuss much anymore. Sin was treated mostly as an embarrassment these days. Miss Budge knew better. Sin was dangerous; it could rob you of an authentic life in Christ. Miss Budge was a repeat sinner and a regular repenter.

She prayed unceasingly, "Lord, save us from ourselves. Save me."

"Ma'am, may I ask your name?" the guard asked with his notepad ready.

"Midriff Bulge," Miss Budge replied, and then winced. "Mildred Budge." She amended. "My name is Mildred Budge."

"I believe you," the officer said. "What did you see?"

Miss Budge considered the question and answered it honestly. "At first, I saw a lady chasing a dangerous man through dangerous traffic for only money. Then I saw people buying stuff they don't need. We are all too busy eating French fries and drinking bad milkshakes to cover up how afraid we are that, if we give up stuff and salt and sugar, there will be nothing left. We are afraid life won't taste good without all this. That lady who chased the crook—she's really afraid."

The guard ignored the way the older woman's mind wandered. Maybe she was growing deaf. "Did you see his face?" he asked slowly and loudly.

Miss Budge smiled ruefully. "He looked like everybody."

The guard put away his notepad, nodded his thanks, and walked back to the victim-hero.

As the waves of fear that had almost made her faint subsided, Miss Budge tossed out her milkshake and fries. She reread her shopping list. She already had the same stuff at home, except for that lipstick called Ruby Woo. Miss Budge was certainly stockpiling, like her mother before her. Sometimes shopping made her feel close to her mama, who had been gone a long time. But the acquisition of stuff filled neither the hole left by her mother's death nor any of the other vacuums in her life. Miss Budge saw that in buying stuff, she was postponing the inevitable. She must face the vacuums—experience emptiness created by the will of God—and try not to fill those holes with substitutes that would taste like a cheap milkshake. She must fill it with the truth of a life lived authentically in Christ by agreeing with him in all things. That's what real repentance was.

"Today," Mildred Budge proclaimed, turning her back resolutely on the store, "I am going to choose a fearless life. I am going to be unafraid of what life feels like without being all covered up or weighed down with stuff that isn't what I truly want."

Determined, Miss Budge tossed her shopping list in the trashcan and marched back to her car. She placed her hands on the steering wheel and explained to God, "I do still want that lipstick called Ruby Woo. You know how I feel about the color red—on its own. I love red." She took a breath and continued, "But I want to wait a while on Ruby Woo. And I want an adventure. What I really want is courage, so I can choose a life free of covetousness. I want to live my life, not consume it. Will you help me?"

And with that prayer in motion, wending its way around her heart, moving in her mind, doctoring her soul, Miss Budge sent her spirit on ahead to her house; and then, she purposefully aimed her car in the same direction.

Commitment Sunday

All the women who owned fur coats did not wear them to church on Commitment Sunday. It was mostly a universal response to the challenge to write down one's financial pledge to the church for the coming fiscal year.

Mildred Budge did not own a fur coat, but not because she didn't want one. There were days when Miss Budge intensely coveted a fur coat, so that she could sit on the sofa in her living room and watch Joan Crawford movies. But she wouldn't spend money on a fur coat that could be invested in missions instead.

Besides, Mildred Budge had lived long enough to know that she wasn't the fur coat type. She wasn't glamorous—didn't look like Joan Crawford or Grace Kelly. Mildred Budge was a little pigeon-breasted, a little pear-shaped, and like many church ladies, she frequently rolled her hair. She liked curls.

Unlike other church ladies, however, Mildred Budge dressed down on Easter Sunday. That was because Miss Budge didn't buy her springtime dress until the week after Easter when finer dresses went on sale.

A woman could always find a high quality dress for half price then. Rather than pay top dollar just to look better one week earlier, Miss Budge waited to dress up and used her Easter dress savings as her Faith Promise pledge.

That strategy wasn't the way the Faith Promise plan was proposed at church.

Mildred Budge had long since given up trying to memorize the formula for having faith that God would supply an extra abundance of money for missions through His members, and when He did, that was supposed to become one's Faith Promise pledge. Only Mildred's faith didn't produce that exact number. She had a reasonable faith that God would give her an Easter dress the week after Easter and that she would save enough in her dress budget to return that as her Faith Promise donation.

The annual pledge made on Commitment Sunday was different. That was a standard 10 percent—before taxes. Your basic tithe. But Mildred didn't like the legalism of that word any more than she liked the words *fiscal year*, since any Christian worth her salt or the price of a ruby could tell you that God didn't measure that way. A tithe was only a good way to start, but it was not a definitive answer to how much was the right amount to give to the church if you were talking about the Master of the universe who had exhaled His own life-giving breath into you, put shoes on your feet, stocked Blue Bell ice cream in your freezer, and gave you a good spring dress each year, just as if you were a lily of the field.

No. You couldn't be a child of God and live like that and believe that tithing was anything more than a place to start. Only 10 percent of her annual income felt dry and too tight to Miss Budge, and when you dressed down in order to write down the words, the pledge felt simultaneously legally accurate and, in her heart, illegitimate. God knew her bank account, and more significantly, what generosity felt like to her. And she knew what joy was from Him. When God happened to Mildred Budge, it was in streams of delight—a kind of manna from heaven—that didn't have a real price tag the way real art doesn't, even though people put prices on it to trade or sell. Grace wasn't for sale or trade.

So, unlike Easter Sunday, Mildred Budge dressed up on Commitment Sunday because she loved any kind of ritual that encouraged family members in a church to think about the family budget. When she confronted the pale blue pledge card, Miss Budge wrote down 10 percent, as always. Then, she thoughtfully added a plus sign (okay, it was a cross), and because she was sentimental (and why had *they* decided sentiment was a second-rate attitude in church?), the dear lady drew a heart around the cross. Hers. And then, in the spirit of renewing her vows of faith, the church lady signed her name: Mildred Budge.

Christmas Right Now

There wasn't much that worried Mildred Budge about Christmas anymore.

She knew Jesus.

Eternity was decided.

For her, a long-time church lady, all the regular holiday festivities were scheduled and logically organized.

Miss Budge knew the date of the annual Lunch Bunch Christmas Brunch.

She knew the recipes for her requested contributions to various fellowship potluck meals.

Other than inventorying her pantry and making sure she had enough brown, white, and confectioner's sugar, there wasn't much more to buy.

She knew what she was giving to her friends: chocolate pecan homemade fudge.

Fran Applewhite got fudge. And Mildred received fingertip towels from her.

Belle Dearborn got fudge. And Mildred received a six-pack of small bottled Coca-Colas. (They lasted her six months.)

Her mailman and her paperboy got fudge; she reliably received her mail and her morning paper year round.

Choosing the fudge-making day was the biggest variable of the holiday season each year, but Miss Budge wasn't worried. You only needed one good cold dry day so the candy would set. There was always a perfect day sometime after Thanksgiving and before Christmas.

This year, she was more concerned about what the newest member of their Lunch Bunch, Anne Henry, might do next.

Anne Henry liked to do things that the other ladies didn't do. She had recently dyed her hair a vivid red, wore eye shadow with glitter in it, and the previous summer she had ridden in a hot air balloon. (No one who worried about breaking a hip and landing in a nursing home did that.)

Anne had danced with a crowd of teenagers at the country club last New Year's Eve. (No one who worried about her dignity did that, either.) Anne Henry was always moving, always busy.

Two days ago, Anne had shown up at Mildred's back door with a nice-sized sack of pecans. "These are for you, Mildred. When you make that first batch of your famous fudge, will you remember me?"

"Where did you get these?" Mildred asked. They weren't from the Tucker Pecan Company. She eyed them suspiciously. Foreign pecans.

"I picked them up on my morning walk. They were like jewels laid at my feet," Anne confessed. "I probably saved the lives of some squirrels. Some of those pecans were dangerously close to the street."

"You picked up pecans from other people's yards?" Mildred asked incredulously.

"Right near the curb. I waved at all the homeowners, and they all waved back. They're absolutely delicious," Anne promised. "I ate a few." Then, she made that little wave she had used on the dance floor and from the air balloon and power-walked away, calling over her shoulder, "Merry Christmas, our Mildred!"

The pecans stayed untouched on the kitchen table while Mildred worked on her calendar, writing additional chores beneath her holiday social engagements, because one didn't just show up somewhere—one had to prepare to get there. It's what made the Christmas season work. All church ladies knew that.

On a separate sheet of paper, then she made additional notes: wash the car and practice the piano.

Mildred had been practicing playing Christmas carols since the pianist three years ago had not shown up for the candlelight service. Fearing he would have to lead the singing a cappella, the preacher had called out to the congregation in what sounded like a cry for a doctor, "Is there a pianist in the house?"

If her sweet minister had only used a different word, Mildred would have marched heroically right to the piano and saved the day, but Mildred Budge did not think of herself as either a pianist or a hero.

Anne Henry didn't stop to think of herself at all. She had simply gone over to the piano and hit as many wrong notes as right ones, and people had good-naturedly sung louder to cover her mistakes. What a joyful noise!

When the service was finished, the preacher escorted Anne Henry to the front of the congregation, bowed respectfully, and lightly kissed the top of Anne Henry's hand.

Since then, Mildred Budge had practiced playing Christmas carols throughout the year in case the preacher ever needed help again.

She had been dancing, too. Thinking about Anne dancing, Mildred danced during the commercials played on TV. She was trying to build up her dancing stamina in case the opportunity arose again the next year.

It probably wouldn't.

Chances to dance and save the preacher didn't come around too often.

Chores done and the TV turned off, Mildred finally sat down heavily at her kitchen table. Her hand toyed with the bag of pecans. One of the plump nuts peeked out of its shell. Mildred pinched it off. Tasted it. Tender. Sweet. Perfect. A jewel. Mildred popped it in her mouth. Delicious! Mildred dialed Anne's number.

Anne picked up the phone immediately. (Anne was famous for not screening calls.) Miss Budge exclaimed, "This is the day that the Lord has made. Let's rejoice and be glad in it!"

"You're making the Christmas fudge!" Anne deduced instantly. Before Mildred could explain that she had been calling to thank her properly for the nuts, Anne said, "I'll come right over and help you!"

"Now?" Mildred asked tremulously, looking around the kitchen.

Making the candy was not on her day's schedule. The nuts weren't even shelled. She hadn't even seriously prayed over her ingredients. Was rain predicted?

"You're giving me Christmas right now, aren't you?" Anne pressed, and there was excitement in her voice. It was the same tone she had used to call down greetings from the air balloon. It was the same exuberant joy that flooded the dance floor the previous New Year's Eve.

Tears sprang to Mildred Budge's eyes. It was the first time anyone had ever called time spent with Mildred Christmas.

As if she were saying yes to the preacher's cry for a pianist, Mildred Budge replied bravely, her feet doing a little practice jig at the prospect of accepting this unplanned gift of the season, "Yes! Come on over, Anne. Let's you and I have Christmas right now."

The Martha Problem

Mildred Budge knew she had a problem with serving others. She just didn't know how to solve it.

She didn't mind caregiving of any kind; it was just the opposite. Mildred Budge couldn't stop from trying to be helpful.

Just the other day at a church fellowship lunch, she had reached over and cut up the meat on the plate of a deacon. He had glared at her and said, "I can feed myself and tie my own shoes."

Miss Budge had slunk away to the kitchen where she had overheard two people talking about women who had so little self-respect that they couldn't stay out of the kitchen. She was pretty sure they were talking about her. She dropped off her dirty dishes—fought the fierce desire to wash them herself—then left, feeling pale.

But the final moment of conviction that she needed to modify her Martha-esque impulses occurred after she happened upon a family from out of town who had been involved in a car accident.

Naturally, she stopped, called a tow truck for them, and invited them to her home for a cooked lunch, which was Samaritan-okay. But then, feeling a rush of ecstasy over the perfection of her steaming cornbread, which really did turn out superbly, Miss Budge couldn't let hot buttered cornbread with black-eyed peas be enough. No! At the end of the meal, she asked, "Would you like a tour of Montgomery while you are here?" After all, they were on vacation and sitting in her house was not exactly the same thing as having a good time.

Taken aback, the family of four had turned down her offer to go see F. Scott Fitzgerald's house; the First White House of the Confederacy; the church on Dexter Avenue, where Martin Luther King Jr. had found his voice for the civil rights movement; and the Alabama Shakespeare Festival. Instead, overwhelmed by the offer of so much culture, the daddy had asked for a phone book and called a taxi to take the four out-of-towners to the garage where their car was in the process of being repaired.

Miss Budge didn't blame them. When you have been in an accident in a city not your own, you don't want to see the sights. Mildred didn't even know why she had made the offer, because deep down, she had not wanted to drive them to all of those places.

But she had offered, and now she was left with the persistent questions that plagued women like her and Martha from the Bible who fretted over domestic work and frequently pestered others with offers of unnecessary help: *Do I need gratitude? Or is the problem worse?* Miss Budge gulped: *Am I trying to earn grace?*

She didn't know—but sometimes she condemned herself for trying to be more helpful than the occasion merited. She explained herself to Jesus as helpfully as she knew how: "I'm not tired of doing good works, you see; I just want to do the good works appointed for me. I am not tired of running the race set before me, either; I just want to run the race you approve of. I *am* tired," she said, "of being that Martha kind of woman who didn't exactly annoy you, but you did say that Mary chose the better way," she recalled softly. "What is that?"

How could one find that better way? she wondered.

Miss Budge decided to make some decisions that would govern her actions.

Initially, she decided to stop carrying temptation around with her in the form of bottles of water in the trunk of her car, even though she had recently been stuck on the interstate in a traffic jam in hundred-degree heat and was thirsty enough to drink some. In retrospect, it did seem imprudent to have gotten out of her car and walked down the interstate handing out bottles of warm water to other trapped, thirsty drivers.

And, she was going to stop stacking the dirty dishes on her table at restaurants just because the waitress appeared overworked.

And, at fellowship suppers, she would not be the first person to jump up and offer to fetch more coffee or cake for anyone nearby.

And, when she was at the home of another church lady whose turn it was to play hostess, she was not going to pester the appointed Martha-for-the-Day with repeated offers of table service, while six other church ladies sat peacefully at the dining table, graciously allowing themselves to be served. There was a balance to be found in giving and receiving, serving and being served, and Mildred Budge was going to seek, knock, and find it.

That was her initial, prayerful plan, and she concluded it with a solemn promise: "Jesus, I will try to choose the better way that you told Martha existed. She believed you. So do I."

Then, later that very afternoon, as she drove home from her quilting class, Miss Budge saw a beggar standing on the side of the road. As she read the familiar message on the card he held—Will Work For Food—Miss Budge recalled bleakly that she had no bottle of water to hand him and he had to be thirsty. She did have some emergency cash. It wasn't much though.

Hoping that her right hand wouldn't know what her left hand was doing, Miss Budge slowed down, crumpled the ten dollar bill from the glove compartment into a tidy ball, and flipped the money out the window to the fellow who was most likely a drug addict or a con man. (Everyone said that's who those men were, but how was one to know?)

Then feeling unwise, if not a failure, Miss Budge prayed inexplicably, "Jesus, pretend you didn't see that."

Backslid Christian

Mildred Budge liked to get to the church fellowship hall a good hour before the service, so she could put her famous cherry cobbler in the oven to bake during the evening service. Then, even though it was not her official job, Miss Budge double-checked the table arrangements, smoothed the disposable paper tablecloths, patted with her own hands the stacks of white paper napkins to ensure there were enough and extra for the spills that would occur, added two pitchers of ice water to the coffee pot table for the water drinkers who were often overlooked, and then she imagined the evening.

It would be good. Refreshed from worshiping God the Father, Maker of the Universe, the family of God would stand in the twilight of the Lord's Day and sing: "The steadfast love of the Lord never ceases. His mercies never come to an end. They are new every morning, new every morning. Great is that faithfulness, oh, Lord. Great is thy faithfulness."

Then, with the sentiments of longing and affection they all held for Jesus and one another fresh on their lips and newly known in their hearts, they would postpone the weekly good-bye for two hours by walking from the sanctuary to the back fellowship hall to share a covered dish supper.

The church lady inhaled the coming moment, cocking her head, as cars began to steer into the parking lot. Shortly, other ladies and some men would enter the side door, bringing their dishes covered in plastic wrap or foil. These dishes would be placed in the same table spots that had emerged over time as the right places for Lori's Greek salad, Sue's pineapple casserole, and Jennie's banana pudding, which had been Thelma's, but Thelma had died of a brain tumor and the recipe was picked up by Jennie and carried forward in time. You didn't eat that pudding without thinking of both women, and Miss Budge smiled with a growing contentment. Her signature dish was the cherry cobbler. She had been making it for years. It had grown in size from a regular Pyrex dish to a doublewide casserole pan, because—and Miss Budge loved this!—people fought over her cobbler, often standing at the end of the table and scraping out the very last spoonful of cherry filling.

Envisioning that moment, Miss Budge thought it a good idea to turn the coffeemaker on so the brew would be ready to drink with her cobbler. She touched the right button, but no red light flickered on. She tapped it again. Nothing. Leaning over, she looked underneath the table and saw the coffeepot's cord hanging loose, unplugged. That wouldn't do.

Dropping to her knees, Miss Budge leaned and bent and reached, but she couldn't grasp the cord that would bring life to the appliance. Loathe to punish her knees by crawling on them underneath the table, she sat down heavily in her good black slacks on the floor and scooted backward, ducking her head as she went under the table and pushed herself to the outlet. She plugged in the cord just as the side door opened and people entered. Instinctively Miss Budge pulled her legs underneath the table, concluding instantly that, rather than emerge in such an undignified posture, she would simply wait and come out from under the table after the others had gone.

A steady stream of brothers and sisters passed through then, and Miss Budge felt the fool to be trapped underneath the big beverage table in the fellowship hall. Oddly, the longer she was there, the better it felt simply to rest. Someone thought to press the coffeepot button, and the brewing began. The sound of the coffee dripping overhead felt like rain above her and hypnotized her with the rhythm and a message she sometimes forgot: if she hadn't turned on the coffeepot, someone else would have. She didn't have to do it all. She leaned her head back against the cool brick of the wall and vowed to remember that.

The last of the potluckers with dishes to deliver passed through the fellowship hall as the piano in the sanctuary struck the notes of the call to worship. Miss Budge felt obliged to scramble out: but a strange lethargy came over her and, rather than push herself even an inch, she lingered, almost willessly. The unexpected stillness of a voice from deep within her pulsed up from a deep well of her most authentic self and made it to the surface of her consciousness: *Only one thing was ever needed. Is still needed. Choose Me, and everything else will be added.*

Miss Budge inhaled and breathed, "Jesus. Help me to remember."

And she didn't mean that she needed help to remember her cherry cobbler was still in the oven or that one might need to refill those two pitchers of water midway through the supper—the water offered in the name of Jesus himself. She asked God to help her remember Jesus, instead. Simply Jesus. Her Jesus. His name simmered inside of the veteran church lady, calling her to stillness and more stillness, as the recognition of what love and fellowship and worship was and could be.

Fellowship occurred first with Him. Then, His.

Miss Budge's cheek found the cool brick of the wall, and she sagged against it, feeling as if she could die there quite happily.

"Miss Budge, are those your feet?" a man's voice asked.

Brother Steve leaned down and pulled back the tablecloth.

"Yes," Miss Budge replied weakly. "I was plugging in the coffeepot, and I somehow got sidetracked," she explained.

The piano in the sanctuary played louder.

Brother Steve, the preacher, leaned down and offered the church lady his hand.

In charge of the lost and the found, Brother Steve vigorously tugged on Miss Budge until her head was free from the confinement of the refreshment table.

As Miss Budge stood, sand and bits of previous fellowship suppers fell from the back of her second-best black slacks.

"Miss Budge, you appear to be a backslid Christian," he teased, his eyes glowing warmly.

"Oh, I am. I was," she replied easily. "But I have come to my senses," she said, paraphrasing the moment of repentance of the prodigal son.

Inside the sanctuary, the piano called the children from playing outside with "Jesus loves me, this I know."

"After you, Miss Budge," the preacher said, holding the door open that led to the sanctuary.

The church lady passed through, resisting the impulse to curtsy, for she was a great admirer of preachers and could rarely find a way to express that. As she passed him, she began to sing with the other worshipers, who were already standing at their regular places, their mouths wide open, as their hearts spilled out in the declaration that joined them in a truer fellowship than cobbler or hot coffee, "Jesus loves me—this I know."

Fasting on the Fifth Sunday of the Month

"Why don't we fast on the fifth Sunday of the month instead of having our usual brunch?" petite Fran Applewhite proposed. She stood up to speak so that the Sunday school class could see that she was serious.

It was a radical suggestion, proposed by the woman who had introduced using cotton fingertip towels at ladies' luncheons, because they laundered more easily than linen napkins. Fran was also in charge of table arrangements for fellowship suppers. She was an organizational genius about food. Anything to do with eating, Fran was the go-to expert. And, now, Fran was proposing that, instead of the usual fifth Sunday brunch, the women of the Berean Sunday school class not eat at all—but fast instead. "Fast like they do in the Bible," Fran added for emphasis.

And then she sat down.

The Bereans understood the initial benefits of the proposed fast immediately. They wouldn't have to cook and carry food and then clean up afterward. Further, a fast instead of a brunch wouldn't prevent a regular and proper Sunday lunch, which could then occur guilt-free just two hours after the Sunday school hour, when they could in very good conscience break the fast at home or at the country club where, not incidentally, bread pudding with warm whiskey sauce was offered. No one ever mentioned the bread pudding; everyone knew about it.

Impressed with Fran's ingenuity and intrigued by the idea of a radical change in church-lady behavior, the class appeared to be resistant to the idea at first by a collective, thoughtful silence. This first quiet response that could have been mistaken as "no" was really only a sensitive expression of courtesy, just in case there was someone in their midst who really, really wanted to eat brunch on the fifth Sunday.

Time was allowed for this woman to speak up. When she didn't, Anne Henry, who was the local tennis champion and famous for her consistent volleys, rose and asked logically, "What are we going to do if we are not eating or having our regular Sunday school lesson?"

Mildred Budge had been waiting for this moment for some time. Inspired by her friend Fran's courage, she too stood up and proposed, "We could sing praises." Then, in a sudden fervor, Mildred added, "I always wish we could sing more."

"And we could drink glasses of ice water with lemon," Anne Henry suggested thoughtfully, as the idea of not eating on the fifth Sunday began to take hold. "Singing makes me thirsty."

"Ice water with lemon can be very filling, too," the new president of the Sunday school class agreed, with gentle deference that was very becoming. Her humble tone was like the other women's voices in the class. For when women negotiate change, their plans often carry a tinge of mea culpa for thinking out loud.

"I take a diuretic for my blood pressure. I won't be drinking iced water with lemon," the former president of the class replied briskly.

And inappropriately. She had lost the election by a considerable margin to the new president, and refusing to drink a glass of water was a subtle way of expressing her hurt feelings.

"It's entirely optional," the new president replied gracefully, and the class breathed a sigh of relief that she was going to be easy to get along with.

The former president had been a bit contrary from time to time, which she proved by asking aggressively, "Does this fast idea mean we can't eat breakfast at home?"

She looked expectantly at the new president to resolve this theological point, but Fran, who had initiated the discussion, rose protectively and took responsibility for creating the controversial situation.

"It does. Otherwise, you'll be spending your regular Sunday school time just not eating brunch, which is what most of us do anyway on the other Sundays of the month, except for those honey-filled drops that have twenty calories a piece in them that Mildred Budge gives us."

Mildred Budge did not know why Fran brought up the Honees, but Fran was most likely more nervous than she appeared and so had just rambled on thoughtlessly, without realizing that she was in a way setting up Mildred to be criticized for what had always been considered the virtue of generosity.

With a liquid honey center and imported from Italy, Honees were extra special—the perfect piece of candy. "I buy Honees by the case," Mildred confessed recklessly. It was both a confession and a boast. Mildred Budge recognized that paradox in herself and was determined to repent.

As Mildred made that resolution, Fran nodded significantly at her best friend—that familiar quiet glance of friendship that translated, "I don't know why I just said that. Sorry."

Mildred smiled with understanding, and now desperately wanted a Honee, but resisted the impulse to reach for one.

With the mention of the Honees, the minds of Mildred's friends, the Bereans, roamed associatively to John the Baptist and his eating of locusts and honey. Though they were not fasting yet, they were all wondering if they could worm a Honee out of Mildred with a slight cough sometime between that very moment and the next fifth Sunday. Then they would have a Honee safely stored in their purses, just in case this not eating on the fifth Sunday became a desperate situation.

Reading the growing tension among them, Fran stood up again and made another radical suggestion. "Let's pray on the fifth Sunday. Fast if you want to; don't fast if you don't want to! But let's pray when we get here," Fran said.

"Pray the whole time?" the former president asked, snappishly. "For a whole hour?"

The whine in her voice caused the new president to stand again, this time assuming the position of protective authority that was expected of an elected leader. "If we run out of things to pray about, we'll start singing Mildred's hymns," the new president suggested diplomatically. And then, before the situation could get worse, she announced with finality, "That's what we'll do the next fifth Sunday then. Bring your prayer lists from home."

Change had happened. Worrisome, challenging change. Already the individual women could feel the tension created by giving up a routine and, in the giving up, confirmed their collective desire for spiritual growth.

But will I have to pray out loud? Or will only those ladies who are comfortable praying out loud do the work for us all?

They were scared, but when the fifth Sunday of the month came, there was an unusual show of attendance. Feeling hungry and disoriented, the women, some with stomachs that didn't usually start growling till the preacher started to speak an hour later, attempted to muffle the sounds by hurriedly drinking ice water with lemon provided by the new president. Then, one by one—standing to pray—and with less apology in their voices than usual, they began to open their mouths and confess a need for God and his providential care that was deeper than their ten-minute prayer routine, usually allowed before the once regularly scheduled fifth Sunday brunch.

They prayed without ceasing. They prayed for the salvation of souls—for nieces and nephews and neighbors they confessed they didn't like. They asked God to help them love their neighbors as themselves. Tears fell.

The new class president petitioned for increased patience with one another. Her voice broke. The former president passed her a Kleenex.

Then, Anne Henry urged good sportsmanship among the sisters.

Fran interceded for mercy.

Mildred Budge thought of the whiskey sauce on the bread pudding at the country club five times before she finally stood up and prayed, "Give us, Lord, our daily bread, and let us be truly grateful." She meant it.

Yes, the fast, like most of Fran's ideas, was a great move toward something that was hard to define: holiness.

The ladies felt a hunger to pray that they had not known before, and a strange desire to give up different types of food ministries that had felt (though they hadn't stopped to talk about it before) sometimes like busy work rather than real help that was really needed.

Delighted that they could be challenged and change, the Berean church ladies agreed to not eat together again on the next fifth Sunday. And as they passed

Mildred Budge, they stifled both real and nervous coughs, while Mildred wrestled with the temptation to reach into her purse.

Mildred Budge did not give out any Honees that day, nor would she ever again on any fifth Sunday of any month. It was for her a different kind of fast: a personal response to a personal challenge. Like any call to radical change, not giving out candy was strange at first for Mildred Budge, then liberating; and ultimately, the small shift in her thinking felt undeniably right.

Onward Christian Soldiers

Mildred Budge stopped in her tracks when she read the words on the yellow flyer hanging from the telephone pole outside the church: "Come enjoy a delicious breakfast and gourmet coffee in the Disciples Class."

It was unbelievable. She shook her head and kept walking, only to see another yellow flyer, just like the other one, posted on the next pole that lined the sidewalk leading into the church building.

Fran came up behind Mildred Budge and read the words over her shoulder. "I've never seen anything like that in my life. I mean, every now and then the choir tries to recruit new members with food—and someone calls my house about twice a year and says they want me to come sing in the choir because they like the way I sing in the pew."

"You don't sing that well," Mildred said, squinting to see if Fran thought otherwise.

"Of course I don't. Well, anyway, this thing right here—this sign, this yellow thing," she sputtered. "It's worse than the choir calling late at night after I was already in bed and having a really good dream." The late-night call from a volunteer with the choir trying to recruit new members was still a sore subject with Fran. There were written rules and there were unwritten rules, and inside the church, not calling after nine o'clock at night unless someone had died fit in the latter category: you didn't do it. So did posting yellow flyers. Fran reached over and ripped it off. "I think we need to have a pow-wow with the other girls."

Mildred nodded, thinking that the timing was bad, because the Berean Sunday school class had only recently switched, after a hundred years of eating brunch together on the fifth Sunday of the month, to fasting instead and praying for the sick and the lost instead of chowing down. It had been a big deal that had happened easily, and Mildred was curious about what might happen next in Sunday school if they found themselves in competition with the Disciples, who were now using a traditional church lady ministry of food to woo others to their classroom.

Fran and Mildred walked in together, down the first hallway that led to the classroom, where the all-woman Sunday school class met. The smell of coffee perking permeated the rooms and the hallway, and the sound of pianos tinkling here and there throughout the Sunday school wing proved that someone—a sister in the faith usually—was getting ready to lead her particular class in a praise song before getting down to studying the Bible—what Sunday school was really about.

Anne Henry was standing in the doorway of their classroom holding another advertisement, and when she saw Fran's, she waved hers and whispered incredulously, "Gourmet coffee!"

Women who had not wanted to give up the brunch on the fifth Sunday congregated around Anne, who was shaking her head, "We're going to have to do something about this. No doubt about it."

"Why?" Mildred asked. "If that class wants to cook breakfast and try to get new members to join their Sunday school class, what is that to us?"

Anne Henry rolled her eyes and gave Fran a look that said, *Explain it to her, will you?*

"Mildred, now you know that women have a reputation as rubies to show hospitality," Fran said. "It's not only about the cooking; it's about being ready to serve. To anticipate needs. To have the stuff other people want." Fran held up her handbag and shook it. The loot inside made a comforting sound. "Yours is the same way. You're loaded with Kleenex, aspirin, cough drops—those imported Italian candies with a little drop of honey in the middle for a raspy throat—and all the stuff that anyone could need, and—"

"Let me put it another way, Millie," Anne Henry jumped in. "We're the equivalent of Christian Marines. There's the army and the navy, and then there is the Marines, the ones they count on to hold down the fort when there's no one else. That's us." It was a statement that one had to take on faith, because, unlike a Marine,

Anne Henry was very glamorous; she was even wearing some Nancy Pelosi-like pearls, though she didn't like for people to call them that.

"And now, some newbies in the Disciples class are offering a hot breakfast ..." Anne Henry said.

"It's got to be frozen biscuits microwaved. That's all it can be," Fran conjectured.

"What about this *gourmet* coffee?" Anne Henry asked.

The ladies turned and eyed their own familiar coffee urn that was ready for them each week. Somewhere in the building was a deacon who made the coffee for all the Sunday schoolers. No one knew exactly who he was because he wanted to keep his right hand from knowing what his left hand was doing, but he made pretty good coffee: not too weak—not too strong. And he was faithful. It was always ready.

Offering and drinking something called gourmet coffee was a slap in that good deacon's face; it was as simple as that.

"I hope the church isn't paying for gourmet coffee," Fran said. She was a staunch proponent of conservative fiscal stewardship, and gourmet coffee was reckless spending. Before anyone had a chance to theorize, Fran answered her own question: "Surely not. Surely they're taking up a collection and buying it themselves. Probably Starbucks from the grocery store. What else could it be?"

"You don't suppose they have one of those machines that drips espresso into those little white cups?" Mildred asked.

"Well, if they do, that's going too far. I know that," Fran said.

"Where exactly is the Disciples' classroom?" Mildred Budge asked, sniffing. She liked espresso very much. If she could have carried around a little cup of it in her purse, she would have.

Anne Henry and Fran smiled at the same time. While the flyer was impressively prepared—the words were spelled correctly and everything—someone had forgotten to name the location of the Disciples' classroom. No one said a word out loud. Not one of the Bereans was indiscreet enough to point out that kind of speck in another Disciple's eye.

Instead, Anne balled up her flyer first, and then Fran copied her. They tossed the flyers in the trashcan and laid down their capacious purses so they could pour cups of average coffee from the same urn they always used, and which one of them kept washed on the Q.T., because it had been discussed that, while a man might very well be able to make coffee, he couldn't clean a coffee pot the way a woman would. In order not to hurt his feelings, one of the women cleaned the coffee urn sometime during the week and then put it back where the deacon expected to find it.

"Well, if we ever revisit that idea about brunch on the fifth Sunday, maybe we'll put up a flyer too and add the room number," Anne suggested.

It was spoken. That was how a member of the Berean Sunday school class suggested that a previous decision that had been made and tried was now up for reconsideration.

It would never even come to a vote. Without a formal discussion and without a formal vote (for that could prove awkward), the next fifth Sunday of a month, the Berean women would arrive with their signature dishes and create a hospitable buffet of egg and sausage casserole, cheese grits, bacon biscuits, mixed fruit salad, blueberry muffins, banana bread, and juices with coffee, only regular coffee, but served hot from a clean urn.

Before it even happened, each woman in the room who had voted to fast changed her vote and everyone knew it. Each woman started planning the menu of what she would personally bring and serve.

The women all looked at each other wordlessly.

"When did we start advertising Sunday school—that's what I'd like to know?" Fran demanded to know.

"Is that the same thing as testifying?" Mildred asked.

Fran shook her head. Anne touched her Nancy Pelosi beads, a strand of large pearls in a variety of colors that all matched somehow. It was pretty, pretty, pretty.

Mildred coveted them, and then did the equivalent of plucking out her envious eye: she closed her peepers and tried to shake away the image of how pretty those pearls were.

Fran sat down and took a thoughtful sip of her coffee. When the next fifth Sunday of the month approached, they might very well post a flyer, too. *What color should it be? Not yellow. Not pink; the members of the class were past the pink stage. What color is a Berean?* Fran wondered.

Mildred leaned over and whispered to Fran, "I guess not everybody wanted to fast after all."

"It was mainly you, Mildred," Fran said flatly, without looking at her friend. "We were all just trying to please you." She didn't add: Yes, I stood up and said the words but I was speaking for you. Look where it's gotten us now.

Rebuked, Mildred sat back in her chair thinking one more time soberly: *It's a big job, this—working out one's salvation with fear and trembling. The Bible advises fasting. Really it does.* Mildred thought the words, but she did not say them.

"And our flyer will have the classroom location on it," Fran declared, as she blew on her coffee. Fran blew more than she sipped.

Anne Henry walked over to the piano and opened the hymnal and began to rifle the pages, looking for an anthem to kick off the class, as other members arrived— some holding foreign cups with gourmet coffee discovered in a different classroom where they had stopped on their way to their home class. Anne Henry saw the foreign cups.

Temptation took many forms. So did betrayal.

Taking a deep breath, she called out, "Shall we sing 'Onward Christian Soldiers?'"

It was a rallying cry, a unifying anthem, a reminder that in their way, church ladies are the Marines.

The members of the class nodded with conviction, and holding their different cups of coffee, began dutifully to sing.

Turkey Dog

"What are you doing for Thanksgiving?" Mildred Budge asked the newest member of the Lunch Bunch, which was something of a secret society of single veteran church ladies that had been meeting once a month for Sunday lunch for years. Members had come and gone, but the Lunch Bunch as an entity had outlasted many preachers, even the ones who preached against eating out on Sunday.

Mildred Budge agreed with preachers about not causing other people to work by eating out on Sundays, but she ate out anyway. It was a compromise that she believed proved she was in the reformed tradition but had avoided becoming legalistic.

Mildred figured that love expressed through fellowship after church on Sunday covered the potential trespass elements of eating out—which no matter how you looked at it, didn't really fit into the category of pulling a cow or an ox out of the mud (one of the approved reasons for not resting completely on Sunday)—but it worked for Mildred and this new member of the Lunch Bunch, Betty, of whom Mildred had just asked an entirely inappropriate question. "What are you doing for Thanksgiving dinner?"

Unless she knows a woman very well and also the answer, a seasoned unmarried church lady does not casually ask another sister-in-the-faith what she is doing for Thanksgiving. There are many reasons why.

Quite simply, if asked of a single lady or a widow, the question indelicately points out her aloneness. More troubling, the question implies that you are about to invite her to your house; and one more time, Mildred had decided that she wasn't cooking a big meal for Thanksgiving and inviting her gal pals over. No, each year, she now accepted one of the invitations that came her way from people who saw her as someone who shouldn't be eating alone. Thanksgiving with acquaintances was Mildred's newest Thanksgiving tradition.

Betty, an athletic older woman who was famous for working out with weights at Gold's Gym (she had muscles in her triceps), stared distantly out in space—her eyes a luminous, lucid blue—and said, "I would like to be eating a turkey dog on Thanksgiving."

"That would be a hot dog made out of turkey?" Mildred confirmed, wondering if she needed to cancel her plans and invite Betty over to her house anyway, no matter how much work it was.

Betty collected herself, read Mildred's mind, and added quickly, "Don't worry about me. I have a few Thanksgiving invitations, but I have not chosen which one to accept." Betty inhaled deeply and then sighed. Her usual serene expression wavered as she signaled to the waiter that she was ready for her check. Mildred motioned "Me, too." The rest of the Lunch Bunchers had already left for their Sunday afternoon naps. Only Betty and Mildred were lingering, getting to know each other.

Betty drew her shoulders back and vowed, "But I will. One must participate."

"That's right," Mildred concurred.

"I'd so much rather stay home on Thanksgiving Day, eat a turkey dog, and clean out a closet," Betty confessed, recklessly, and then looked about to see if anyone had overheard. No one cared.

"Wouldn't you though?" Mildred replied. "Or enjoy a movie festival starring Eve Arden or Thelma Ritter." Mildred Budge had a real fondness for women who had played good-natured, sensible, sturdy sidekicks to the more glamorous female lead characters.

The two women nodded in sympathetic understanding, for each was now viewed by various strata in the social world as a person in need of friends and family for the holidays, and neither woman saw herself that way— not even a little bit. But they were skilled in navigating the perceptions of others, even of other Christians, who took the occasion of the holidays to do a good work on them by inviting them over so they wouldn't be alone.

After accepting an invitation, one was often asked to bring a dish, or—if not—was expected to baby-sit while other guests of child-bearing age finished eating the prolonged meal or adjourned to the TV room to watch the Game. Once that started, a single older woman who had been invited over could find herself baby-sitting until late evening. When the new tradition had begun, a family had actually gone off to a movie and left Mildred at their house with four small children. *"You're a retired teacher. This probably feels like home to you."*

Since then, Mildred always, always took a covered dish and parked her car where she couldn't be boxed in. When possible, she chose a chair at the dining table nearest the front door.

"How about you?" Betty asked politely.

"I'm taking cornbread stuffing to a rather large social gathering. It won't be so bad," Mildred said, without conviction.

"Are you supposed to take the gravy, too?" Betty asked, curious. Using a frosty purple-pink lipstick, she applied it without looking in a mirror. Mildred did the same with her Ruby Woo—her signature shade of red lipstick.

"Oh, I was told explicitly and very loudly—"

"As if you were deaf," Betty interjected, putting her lipstick away.

Mildred nodded, "Not to use cream of mushroom soup either."

"How else does one make gravy without cream of mushroom soup?" Betty asked. She folded her napkin on the table and nodded discreetly to the hovering waiter that he could take her money. Mildred had laid down cash as well.

The waiter discreetly collected their money and topped off their water glasses without asking. "No rush, girls. Take your time," he murmured.

Mildred fished out an extra dollar to add to the tip for that courtesy, explaining at the same time, "They want real giblet gravy made with corn starch and turkey drippings, which will be tricky because I'm not cooking the turkey."

"That is problematic, since giblets come with the turkey," Betty agreed, wrinkling her nose. "I don't care for giblets. All those little indistinguishable parts can be very unappealing." She pushed back her chair, readying herself to leave.

"I have been researching gravy, and it appears that the secret to making good giblet gravy is to boil an egg and slice it up in there with the giblets. It kind of disguises things," Mildred reported.

"I'll remember that," Betty replied, though the piece of information was not filed in that part of her brain that stored the really important information. It was sent to the more distant memory bank, where one kept information about how to paddle a life raft if one ever finds oneself in a flood. "I guess I'll have to say yes to someone," Betty added with fortitude as she stood up.

"You will," Mildred concurred, taking a deep breath. "But if you wait long enough, all of the traditional side dishes will have been assigned to others, and then you can take what you like to cook. It's a good idea to take something," Mildred urged, wondering if Betty understood about the baby-sitting problem. Mildred didn't know yet exactly how long Betty had been on her own. She was a widow.

"That would be a turkey dog," Betty said impishly. "Although I suspect I will just take my cranberry sauce made with Grand Marnier."

"Ah, you like to torment the teetotalers," Mildred said with a grin.

"Just a smidge," Betty said. "But all of the alcohol burns off," she said with a shrug.

"Pity," Mildred replied. She stood up too.

They navigated their way through the restaurant toward their respective vehicles.

When they exited, sunlight flooded them. They blinked while reaching for matching pairs of sunshades that fit over their respective eyeglasses. (All the Lunch Bunch girls wore them!)

They hesitated before parting—each woman alone with her notions about the day ahead and the days ahead. Mildred paused to consider why she still said yes to invitations that were not exactly fun, and knew instantly that it was because she was—in truth just as others saw her—alone, and she did prefer to be with others.

Unfortunately, dining with acquaintances reminded her acutely of the people she loved best who had passed on and were no longer eating at her own carefully laid-out dining room table, smiling and teasing her about cooking with sherry or Grand Marnier. The emotional pall that hovered throughout the holidays threatened to descend.

"Tell me about that turkey dog," Mildred said, wondering if it was too late to invite Betty to her house for an easy meal of turkey dogs. She envisioned open-faced turkey dog sandwiches covered with cream of mushroom soup and watching a Thelma Ritter festival, beginning with *Rear Window.*

Betty grew coy, and her gaze became distant again, matching her voice. "You buy turkey dogs at the grocery store in the cold-cut section. They're right next to the kosher dogs."

Mildred laughed as she read Betty's mind. "You were afraid there for a minute that I was going to invite you to my house for Thanksgiving," Mildred accused, her brown eyes brimming with amused understanding.

Betty looked away, uncomfortable, caught in the act of avoiding someone else's hospitality, even that of a fellow Lunch Buncher.

"I *was* thinking about inviting you," Mildred admitted. "But I really am expected at that family gathering, and I'm really going to take that stuffing and some kind of gravy. I shall bake a chicken at my house and use the delicacies from that as a substitute for turkey giblets. They won't know the difference," Mildred said. "It is very nice to be remembered and asked," Mildred added with determination.

Betty nodded. "I miss my husband," she confessed softly. Then her shoulders went back again, as if she remembered that she must stand up. Stand up very tall. "That was then; this is now," she said, and Mildred knew that her new friend had walked a million miles on that mantra.

Betty looked about for where she had left her car, and found it.

"Sometimes there is laughter at the table," Mildred reminded her.

Betty revolved and smiled with discipline. "Yes, sometimes there is laughter."

"Look on the bright side." Mildred urged, readying her car keys. "When you get home afterward, you can still clean out the closet."

"It is something to look forward to," Betty concurred with a hearty laugh. "And I shall look forward to it and to the many other daily tasks still set before us—with thanksgiving."

A Christmas Treat

Mildred Budge loved the scent of the cinnamon brooms sold in the floral department of her grocery store at Christmas time.

Miss Budge couldn't buy one and take it home because the dense smell of cinnamon choked her and made her eyes burn. But for a passing few seconds, pushing her grocery cart by the decorative brooms in the store, she could inhale and sniff—and let the cinnamony aroma take her back in memory to previous shared Christmases and ahead to the next one.

Near to the cinnamon brooms were silk autumn leaves one could buy on stalks and use for decoration. Miss Budge liked them. Her hand caressed the yellows and browns and reds—colors too vivid to be real. Some people bought them and took them home and placed them in umbrella stands by the front door. Miss Budge didn't. She didn't need to own them. It was enough that the colorful silk leaves were there and her hand could touch them as she passed by and confirm that here it was again: Christmas was coming.

Next to the stalks of decorative leaves were the first red candied apples sealed in the clear plastic forms that were too tightly sealed for ladies' hands to separate.

Miss Budge wouldn't risk breaking a seven hundred dollar porcelain crown on hard cinnamon coating, anyway, even if she could open the package. But they were pretty—those candied apples, and someone would eat them, and it made Miss Budge happy to think that someone could enjoy the sharp tang of a Granny Smith apple combined with the chewy cinnamon candy.

Around the aisle's corner—if not today, then soon—there would be shelves of baking goods: candied fruit, walnuts, pecans, evaporated milk, confectioner's sugar, vanilla extract, and, most likely, peppermint oil.

Miss Budge still stored a bottle of peppermint oil in her cabinet from a disastrous experiment from two years ago, when she had tried to make dark chocolate peppermint patties at home. The candy-making experiment had burned up her hand mixer. Worse, the candies were inedible—too thick from cream cheese that didn't blend. Something had been missing in the recipe, but Mildred Budge did not care enough about the mystery to try and solve it. She loved peppermint patties, but she didn't need to try and make them again.

That wasn't true of other dishes. She had tried many times through the years to make her mother's signature sweet potato pie. But Miss Budge had not succeeded in the twenty years since her mother had passed away. She took an odd comfort in failing in her attempts to duplicate that special recipe. The end result of her cooking experiments told the truth—that no one could make her mother's pies for the holidays like her mother had baked them. The pang of loss was the part of feeling at home during the holidays that contained that blend of sweet pain: true love and true loss, stillness in the midst of great activity, and a fulfillment in Jesus and a yearning for Him that was a paradoxical truth of a Christian's life.

Through the years, Miss Budge had acclimated herself to that encroaching way of wanting and not having that didn't feel like loss, regret, or even loneliness. She had absorbed yearning into her daily life; its presence did not translate untruthfully into self-pity. She was not shortchanged. Satisfaction in what Jesus had supplied for her life was true; yearning for more of Jesus as her very life was also true. She found that the holidays were not the enemy to be conquered—as some warned in discussions about Christmas blues or Christmas giving and spending. Rather, wanting and not having, desiring and learning how to be satisfied, whatever her lot, continued to become part of her growing tradition.

Miss Budge stopped in front of the dairy case and reached for a pint of eggnog. She would let herself have a nightcap of two or three sips for as long as the pint of cold, nutmeggy mixture lasted. It would be enough for many nights of toasting the season, while sitting under an electric blanket and peering through her front window at the wintry stars.

Satisfied with her purchases, she carried her small bag of groceries to the car, surprised that dusk had fallen. She smiled at the first glimpse of the moon that showed up before 5:00 p.m. in her hometown. The turns on her route home were automatic, simple. Red lights turned to green and back again.

At the corner of the last intersection, before Miss Budge steered toward her neighborhood, she caught a glimpse of a flashing light in the small doughnut shop window and her heart leapt up. The message read: Hot Doughnuts Inside Now.

Oh, to eat a hot doughnut instead of a bowl of corn flakes or soup for supper. She made a spontaneous right turn and parked easily by the door of the doughnut shop. The nip of cold in the air brought a rush of pleasure to her eyes, and Miss Budge fastened the top button of her red wool coat and took her place in the stream of people who wanted hot doughnuts too.

Though people respectfully turned to urge the smiling lady to go ahead of them, she declined. For Miss Budge, part of the pleasure of the season was to wait with other people in line for whatever they were all taking their turn to reach. The doughnut line moved slowly. Decisions were important and difficult, and there was so much to see: doughnuts with pink or chocolate or white icings, and rainbow sprinkles, and the very dear ones that had a small blink from which raspberry jelly oozed.

Miss Budge's hand pressed against her heart as she reveled in the color red—her preferred color above all others—but she would not buy the jelly doughnut. Raspberries got in her teeth. The glaze from lovely warm doughnuts did not.

It was too late in the day to eat more than one hot doughnut—too late in the day to drink hot black coffee, too. Miss Budge gulped and said, casting prudence aside, "Two hot doughnuts please, and a cup of black coffee. Is it fresh?" she asked as wisdom attempted to seduce her to the mature choice of eschewing caffeine.

"It's always fresh here," the clerk boasted, spinning energetically to go to the back room where the small, iced, hot doughnuts progressed slowly on the conveyor belt, sugar puddling and dripping all around them.

Another clerk poured Miss Budge's fresh-brewed coffee, snapping a lid on it as the retired schoolteacher paid out the money from her small black change purse. "Can you imagine me—drinking coffee this time of day?" she asked the clerk.

"I can," the clerk said with a conspiratorial grin. "Be careful. It's hot."

"I will be," Miss Budge promised, as the other clerk returned and offered Miss Budge the small white paper bag with her doughnuts. The doughnut lady leaned forward and whispered so that other customers would not hear, "I put a third doughnut in there —on the house. They're kind of small. But what's better than a hot doughnut dripping in sugar?"

"Absolutely nothing," Miss Budge replied honestly, taking her white paper sack and her cup of hot coffee and going, slowly, slowly—she loved people—past the line of smiling neighbors who were supposed to be at home by now but had been wooed off their routes, like Miss Budge.

Outside, the moon was higher and brighter than it had been fifteen minutes before. The sky was rich with red streaks of sunset and clouds that danced against what would become a darker sky. The wind had picked up, sharpened by a chill that had arrived as the sun went down, and Miss Budge stood there on the sidewalk, as stars pulsed into sight. Uncharacteristically impatient, she reached immediately inside the sack and found the free doughnut to eat first while it was still hot. She took a bite of warm melting sugar that dissolved in her mouth like the delicate manna from heaven sent by God, first to the wandering Israelites, and which had shown up in so many different ways in her own good life. She offered a deep moan of gratitude for the gift of life every day and ate the doughnut gloriously, without regret.

Then, snapping back the small lip of the coffee cup, she took a tentative sip—found it good—slurped three more times, and then she remembered that a small portion was often just the right amount. Miss Budge poured out the rest of the fresh coffee on the parking lot asphalt, like a love offering. Then, she offered another blessing for the chilly night and the bright stars and the sight of candied apples and the smells of cinnamon brooms and the satisfaction of hot doughnuts and the simple joy of spontaneous communion among fellow pilgrims that happened throughout the year, and even between seasons that were not yet wholly Christmas, as it would be one day, ultimately. For every day contained the fulfillment and the yearning that was true in the life of a Christian; and every day of every season contained both the gift of Immanuel's abiding presence and that promise of the next time He will gloriously come.

Beating a Message
of Retreat

As the church was getting ready for its annual all-members retreat, the ladies of the Berean Sunday school class did not sign up.

Even though there were yellow flyers posted all over the church (including the doors of the stalls in the ladies' rooms) informing members how to reserve a cabin at the retreat, the Berean ladies did not sign up.

The church newsletter heralded the benefits of the great opportunity for everyone to retreat together in a relaxed, safe environment, but still Mildred Budge and her veteran Berean church ladies took note only of the recent contributions to the memorial fund. They did not even discuss signing up for the church-wide retreat.

It wasn't because the cooking—at church called the "food ministry"—would have most likely fallen to them. And, sure, young wives, who were still learning that their marriage vows meant surprise and sacrifice and often not enough money, would sob upon their veteran shoulders. The older women, for whom these types of challenges had come and mostly gone, knew that listening was all they could visibly do. Although they would pray later—and that did help—there was a new problem that arose from those encounters: back in the routine of regular church life, the young wives who had told more about their personal lives than they were now comfortable with others knowing, began to duck and hide and, sometimes, they did more than that. Sometimes, the young wives who had talked too much to older women who knew how to keep a confidence would often tease or ignore altogether the older women they had, in a fit of weakness and need, sobbed upon.

The Berean women knew all of that and would have forgiven the slights if they had gotten offended in the first place. But the embarrassed young wives never offended them. Such was the Berean ladies' love for the young women of the congregation that, when the younger women used them or misused them, it was such an understandable human weakness that the Berean ladies did not even report their misuse to one another in search of a corroborating witness who would understand what had happened and take their side. They didn't have a *side* in those kinds of issues anymore; they loved Jesus who had died for them, and they had died to taking offense.

In this way, the Berean women of the church served the congregation in a quiet, loving way that not many people understood. Actually, they were the only ones who understood it. And hence, they understood why they were not, as a group, going on a church-wide retreat.

But because the church leadership wanted 100 percent participation—if not everybody, then a representative from every class, surely!—they sent an evangelist from the church's administration into the Berean Sunday school class. The deacon appeared at the classroom door Sunday morning at 9:45, his chin up, his blue eyes bright with zeal, his backbone stiffened by the myriad warnings from the elder with a gift for administration, who had appointed this newbie shepherd to corral these older ladies who were acting like lost sheep, by delivering a personal invitation to attend the church-wide retreat.

All the women knew the new deacon. Tommy was the grandson of one of their own, and they had loved him since his grandmother, Clovis, announced his birth thirty-three years ago. Many of the Berean ladies had taken turns teaching Tommy in various Sunday school classes when he was a boy. Tommy had graduated from Mildred Budge's public school fifth grade class years before. She had kept a special eye on him—proud, proud of how he had turned out. And now Tommy was a deacon. As he entered the room, Mildred exchanged a proud glance with his grandmother, Clovis.

Tommy cleared his throat before speaking to the class of ladies sitting docilely before him, their legs crossed at the ankles. "We want everyone to come to the retreat and get to know each other in a relaxed setting," Tommy announced vigorously. That was the heart of his message, and he had already delivered it.

When no one objected, his spine elongated, and Tommy spoke more slowly but quite as firmly, the way a new shepherd does, who has his first formal assignment at church and is determined not to fail. Every woman in the classroom was rooting for him. Some prayed.

Throat cleared again, Tommy began: "Dining will be casual, like the dress. And there's plenty of nature and time for walks and meditation and prayer. And it will be a pleasing aroma in God's nostrils if you could all be there to praise the Lord with the rest of the congregation on this glorious church-wide retreat."

Mildred Budge smiled at Tommy and moved her hand in an upward pulsing movement, indicating that he should speak louder. When Tommy spoke again, the ladies in the back could hear him, too. "If one or two of you will sign up, that might help the other women find the courage to follow your example."

Tommy waited for a volunteer.

No women cleared their throats. They didn't look down either. They held his gaze and smiled: they were very proud of him. Tommy was doing a great job!

Mildred scanned the room, wondering who would speak up so that she would not have to be the one to do it. Sometimes, the authoritative role of former teacher undermined a young new deacon's self-confidence.

Fran, Millie's best friend, understood Mildred's concern and tried to explain the class' position to Tommy. "Some time ago, there was a retreat, and all of us went. All of us," she added for emphasis.

To his credit, Tommy nodded, listening—and his mind did not seem to dart ahead, preparing an argument to convince Miss Fran that whatever she was saying was simply an obstacle for him to overcome.

The room relaxed. Idle thoughts occurred: perhaps they could simply tell the young man the whole truth. They waited, though, skilled in silence and let Fran do their talking for them, initially.

"There was in our midst a woman ..." Fran continued.

Tommy nodded discreetly, growing taller and serenely priestlike. His grandmother registered the transformation and wished she had a camera, for Clovis had pictures of her grandson at various stages of his growing up—but never this, never this priestlike composure. Tears filled her eyes, and she fought them as much as she fought saying the words out loud, "That's my boy up there. My daughter's oldest. My heart's darling!"

"And she—like all of us," Fran continued, "was talked into going on a retreat like the one you're planning, and it was a place where there were nature walks, and this woman—younger than we are today—went for an early morning walk to meditate and pray and stumbled and fell down the hillside into a leafy ravine, where she lay for several hours before someone missed her. That is the sad part of the story. No one missed Lucille for several hours."

"Bummer," Tommy commented, and stole a quick glance at his grandmother to see if he should say more. She offered him a discreet, priestlike shake of the head.

Tommy's gaze shifted back to Miss Fran, but now Miss Mildred, who recognized the direction of the truth that Fran had initiated, added—because it was everyone's job to repent—"Eventually, after breakfast, and after lunch, when we were going into the afternoon session, someone said, 'Where is Lucille?' This was the first time one of us had noticed that Lucille was not with us and had not been for many hours."

"That long?" Tommy clarified, and he wondered if that could have happened to his grandmother. A hint of a tear formed in his left eye.

Fran nodded seriously, picking up the thread of the story, as she would have if she and Mildred had planned how to tell it. "We organized a search, and it wasn't hard to find her. Lucy had been calling for help, but no one else on the retreat had gone to walk through nature and pray and meditate on God's glory."

"But all of us searched for her," Mildred interjected, "and we found Lucille and called the paramedics. They came and took a stretcher down to where she was. Lucille was a heavy woman, and they had a difficult time bringing her back up the hillside, which was, if you can understand this, humiliating for her. Lucille left the church after that—I don't think from embarrassment but from having justifiably hurt feelings—"

"No one noticed she was missing until after lunch," Tommy concluded soberly, looking around the room at the number of women who wondered if she had been the one to fall, would she have been left alone? Calling for help? With no one hearing her or missing her for hours?

"There are very few things in my life that have continued to cause me ongoing pain, but that does," Mildred added as well-coiffed Berean heads around the room nodded gently. For the women were steeped in the tradition of silence and repentance; and though they knew the gifts of forgiveness and grace, they retained a righteous sorrow about what had happened to Lucille.

"Poor woman, I don't know what would be worse: falling down a hill like that, or being brought back up on a stretcher slowly because you're heavy?" Tommy mused, and his grandmother wanted to reach out and trace the shape of his face, as she had when he was a boy, and move a lock of thick brown hair off his forehead. But that had stopped between them years ago— at least for him. In her mind, Tommy's grandmother often touched his face and moved that lock of unruly hair.

"It was a wake-up call," Fran added, unexpectedly, and Mildred cast her an approving glance. "We don't go on retreats now—not as penance over Lucille. But because they are—if you will excuse me for saying so, Tommy dear—not right for us. Can you see that? "

Tommy thought about the number of women in front of him who might try to hike while praying, could fall down, and he agreed with them instantly. "I understand exactly what you are saying, and thank you for telling me about poor Miss Lucille. But as the messenger,

I wanted to make sure that you knew that you were all invited to come on this retreat."

"We know we're welcome, Thomas," Anne Henry said, rising and moving vigorously toward the podium. It was time for the announcements to be finished so that they could study the Bible.

Tommy stepped to the side and explained, "It was just that after your class initially declined to participate in the six-week workshop on peacemaking that was part of our campaign for church-wide unity we thought perhaps a second chance at saying yes to this retreat might be a welcome opportunity for you."

"Oh, we enjoyed the six-week workshop on peacemaking," Anne Henry said, and the other ladies nodded their heads vigorously.

"One should be a peacemaker, no doubt about it," Fran interjected enthusiastically. "And Oscar did a most excellent job of telling us how to face conflict and resolve it …"

Tommy had a vague recollection of something Oscar had said after the second week of teaching the Bereans. *"It's like going in there with two years of high school French and trying to teach French to native speakers who have served a lifetime as foreign diplomats."*

"Ladies, thank you for hearing me out. If you change your mind …" Tommy added gallantly. He was feeling heady with the accomplishment of delivering his message and euphoric that it was over.

"A retreat is something for people who are too busy and have too much noise in their lives. We aren't too busy, and we're already quiet," Anne Henry explained.

Tommy eyed Miss Anne with fresh interest, wondering what it would be like to live one's life as a retreat so that special-occasion retreats that cost $87.00 a night would be redundant, but his to-do list beckoned. He had to report to the head man, now that the ladies had said no to the retreat; but the good news was that he didn't think they were mad about anything. Nobody's feathers were ruffled and needed to be smoothed.

Mildred Budge smiled and wondered what it would be like to a tell a young man the whole truth, instead of just part of the truth. She was a big believer in telling the truth; but in this instance, there was quite a lot of it, and Tommy was young. He was old enough to understand about a woman falling down a hillside, but perhaps not old enough to know the kinds of physical challenges that women their age lived with and the state of their sleeplessness and that, when they did sleep, they often snored.

A woman had her modesty. It was one thing to admit to falling down, but having the whole church know how loudly you snored and how often you had to find the common restroom in the middle of the night—well, that was more than any woman wanted anyone outside their Sunday school class to know.

"Mildred, Thomas has turned out to be such a good boy," Anne Henry said, after Tommy closed the door behind him. She adjusted the microphone in order to call for the prayer requests.

Mildred nodded, for she was accustomed to people complimenting her on various members of the church and the community, simply because they had graduated from her fifth grade class years ago. "Tommy is sweet," Mildred agreed. "And brave, too," she added, nodding proudly to Tommy's grandmother. They exchanged congratulatory glances that their combined efforts had resulted in this boy, this deacon, this Tommy.

"Oh, it is brave of him to come here and talk to a bunch of women ..." Anne Henry said, smiling. "Let's add the retreat to our prayers today. It will be good for so many people," she agreed peacefully.

Down the hallway, Tommy caught up with the man in charge, who listened to his report from the Berean class, and said, "Those Berean women just aren't team players."

Naptime on the Prayer Chain

When the phone rang on a Sunday afternoon during universal-after-morning-church-and-before-vespers nap-time, Mildred Budge assumed the reason for the call had to be an emergency or a wrong number.

It was not a wrong number. It was Anne Henry calling by special request for one of their own: a request so urgent that the prayer for mercy needed to be said before Monday morning or even evening worship.

"Liz has asked," Anne Henry said, clearing her throat, even as Mildred Budge grasped her own in a habitual mannerism of stroking her throat when she was concerned about what she was going to have to say—or hear. "That we pray that a man in her neighborhood who rides a bicycle will not fall in love with her."

"She has asked for prayer for that?" Mildred clarified, as her hand moved to her forehead to rub the place between her eyes where the memory of an interrupted nap still lingered. Her heart was racing, and there was a shimmying feeling in her legs, because the phone ringing sometimes caused a start of anxiety: *Who's hurt? What's happened?*

And now this emergency activation of the prayer chain, during the Sunday afternoon naptime, which everyone respected, was being interrupted by Liz, who was afraid a man on a bicycle was going to fall in love with her the next day. Did love happen that fast? If so, what was Liz afraid of? Surely, after three marriages and three funerals, Liz knew how to handle a man on a bicycle.

"Will you call your people and pass along the prayer request?" Anne Henry asked, her voice a study in neutrality.

Anne Henry didn't judge others; she simply didn't. Mildred admired Anne Henry.

However, something in Mildred balked.

"Are you still there?" Anne Henry asked. Mildred heard the rustle of a piece of paper. Her friend had other calls to make before she could lay her head down for an afternoon snooze.

"I'm here," Mildred said with a sigh. She eyed the yellow sofa where she had recently been noodling in a quasi-slumberous state that was the tenor of Sunday afternoon, where resting was the occupation of those who submitted to the commandment to rest: naps were good.

"You've got Fran and Belle on your list."

"I do," Mildred confirmed. "And, let me get it straight: I am supposed to call and pass along the request that a man on a bicycle *not* fall in love with Liz."

Still fresh from reading the long list of the very sick that was passed out church-wide that morning to the entire congregation, Mildred could not help but think that there were more urgent needs of the congregation. The chronically ill. The homebound. The expectant mothers. The soldiers and their families whose names were listed on the same sheet.

Fearing that she could no longer sound unaffected by the content of the prayer request, Anne Henry nodded yes into the telephone. Mildred heard Anne Henry's silence and respected her all the more for it. "I shall pass along the request," Mildred Budge said with finality.

The phone clicked discreetly in her ear, and Mildred inhaled of Anne Henry's decorum. Then, she punched in Fran's number and reported the prayer request. "Liz is afraid a man on a bicycle is going to fall in love with her."

"I've heard," Fran said. "Poor thing. Hers is a difficult life to live."

"Indeed," Mildred agreed.

"But while I have you on the phone, perhaps you would remember that I am singing a solo this evening at church and I am—well, this is silly, I know—I'm afraid of cotton mouth. You know my mouth goes dry when I get nervous."

"Do you want me to pray that you make spit?" Mildred asked, and she felt Fran grin.

"That would be a most excellent prayer," Fran said, clearing her throat.

Mildred hoped Fran would not practice herself hoarse before the evening hour of worship.

"'Twill be done," Mildred said. "Get some rest. I have to call Belle."

"Would you mind calling Carol while you're at it? She's on my list, but I don't have time to talk to Carol this afternoon because I must practice my solo."

Mildred eyed the couch longingly. The Bible verse repeated itself in her memory: "If a man asks for your shirt, give it to him; if he wants you to walk a mile, go twain."

"Yes, I'll call Carol. I'm waking people up."

"That is the nature of love," Fran replied mysteriously, and hung up.

Mildred called Belle next.

"I heard," she confirmed, while Mildred wondered why they needed a formal prayer chain—the grapevine seemed to work pretty effectively. "I'll pray for the man on the bicycle," Belle promised sunnily. It was her signature mood: sunny.

"Fran's singing tonight. You might remember her, too," Mildred added. Fran was her best friend, and the prayers of a righteous woman—or two—availed much.

"Fran will be all right," Belle said dismissively. "I'm going to the church early and placing a glass of water for her on the organ."

Everyone who knew Fran knew she had dry mouth when she sang. Glasses of water abounded in the name of Jesus when Fran sang.

"Good," Mildred said, hanging up.

One more call to make.

Mildred dialed Carol's number, and before Mildred could explain why she was calling, Carol burst out with her news. "I don't care what the emergency is. Mine is worse."

Mildred came to full attention. Carol was a very good link on the prayer chain, and her blast of anxiety was out of character.

"I was just speaking to Genie over at the nursing home, and I told her that if she wants a ride to church tonight, I'll come get her. But she's got to use that lighter aluminum walker, because that one she prefers with the built-in seat is too heavy and hard to fold up and fit in the trunk. It sprang back at me like an accordion last time and almost hit me in the face. It's worse than wrestling a bear."

Mildred cleared her throat to remind Carol that she was calling officially as an activated member of the women's prayer chain.

"I mean it, Millie. Genie's got to make allowances for us. We're all older than we've ever been and that walker she uses to carry her stuff around is too much for us."

Mildred tried to interject, "Liz called—"

"P'shaw. I heard about that. Isn't that Liz bragging that she's about to have another man on her line, like we aren't already convinced that she can get a man. Some women have that knack. I'm the one who's got real trouble. Pray for me. Mildred, I've got an ugly attitude about helping others. I need prayer, and I need it now."

Mildred pretended her hand was holding a pencil, and she mimed writing the words, *I've got an ugly attitude about helping others, and I need prayer.*

"After I told Genie that walker was too much for us, she got mad at me and told me that the walker she took to Sunday service was her business. Well, when you need help from others, it's not all your business, I told her, but she slammed the phone down, and now she's probably going to be distracted by what I said and try not to use any kind of a walker—you know how she tries to do that sometimes? Then, she'll fall over and break something, and it will be my fault."

"No, it won't," Mildred argued, faintly.

"There ought to be a rule about waking everybody up on a Sunday afternoon for a dumb reason like Liz's. Who's in charge of screening prayer requests?" Carol demanded, changing subjects now that her conscience was clear.

"No one," Mildred replied faintly. Her hand mimed writing the words in air: *No one.*

"Well, off the record, and I know we're not supposed to gossip during the prayer chain calls, but I feel sorry for that man on the bicycle. Liz has been a widow three times. Men who marry her seem to die."

Mildred's spine elongated. Her shoulders went back. The room grew brighter. "I suppose we could see this as a life and death situation," Mildred agreed softly, as the idea took shape that Liz, in her way, might be trying to save the life of a stranger.

"Pray for me, Mildred. I'm having a hard time loving others," Carol repeated and hung up.

Miss Budge returned to her sofa and lowered herself thoughtfully. She wondered about all the prayer requests she had heard over the telephone. All the prayer requests she had heard in Sunday school.

She wondered who the man on the bicycle was and how did a woman know when a man on a bicycle who was supposedly going someplace else was about to stop on his journey and fall in love with her? The answers were distant, the paradoxes inscrutable. Yet Miss Budge's spirit was moved.

Activated, with no one needing the shirt off her back or her legs to walk a second mile, Miss Budge recalled what she had heard and imagined what she could not see. Her mouth began to move, and she prayed for the unspoken requests of Anne Henry and for Fran and Genie and Liz and Carol, and, lastly, the man on the bicycle who, if the prayers on the chain worked, she would most likely never meet.

I've Got Your Number

When the phone rang at 6:45 a.m., Mildred Budge almost didn't answer it. She was trying to pray, and that daily discipline was the fuel that energized her days.

Further, she knew who it was disturbing the peace so early in the day; it was a wrong number. The bell sounded ten times and then finally stopped.

Good, Mildred thought. "Now, reverse the last two numbers, dear lady, and try again." Mildred moved out of her prayer time to whisper instructions to the caller she had never met, though she had spoken with Mrs. Henderson several times in the past few weeks—sometimes for a long period of time.

For the occasion of dialing a wrong phone number did not stop Mrs. Henderson from asking Mildred all of the polite questions, and then answering them for herself: "I'm fine, too. Didn't sleep too well last night. Old Arthur is bothering me. Does it look like rain to you, or is my cataract worse?"

Mildred Budge knew that Old Arthur was her caller's name for arthritis. Knew Mrs. Henderson lived alone, ate many bowls of oatmeal, watched the early version of the evening news, and still kneeled down beside her bed before climbing into it alone. Mrs. Henderson also had a cataract, and Mildred Budge wondered who would drive her to the eye doctor to get it lasered. "Let there be someone," Mildred whispered to Jesus, as the phone began to ring again.

With a tip of her head in apology to Jesus for leaving her prayer time, Mildred Budge reluctantly picked up. "It is I, Mrs. Henderson. Mildred Budge. You've misdialed again."

"And how are you, my dear?" Mrs. Henderson asked.

"I am very well indeed. How is your friend with the phone number like mine?" Mildred prompted.

There was a studied pause, as Mrs. Henderson interpreted that information. "Oh, my dear, she is fine, thank you for asking. Is this an inconvenient time?"

"I was simply sitting here having my ..." Mildred almost said "quiet time," but that might have felt like a rebuke to Mrs. Henderson, so Mildred Budge told a partial truth and hoped Jesus would forgive her. "My morning coffee." Well, she was holding a cup of coffee.

"I've had to give up coffee," Mrs. Henderson said. "Too much caffeine makes my nerves hurt."

"Everything in moderation," Mildred replied, picking up her cup. The coffee was cold. Did she want more? Yes, she did.

"I have a pine tree that has died," Mrs. Henderson reported. "It's leaning toward my house."

"I'm sorry to hear that," Mildred replied.

"The tree has been dead since Christmas. I've been watching it. Sometimes big limbs fall."

That worried Mildred. Though she had never seen Mrs. Henderson, Mildred had always envisioned her as a heavy, homebound woman who didn't walk well. Mildred didn't know why she thought this, because one could not tell another's size from her voice alone, but Mildred Budge had always thought of Mrs. Henderson as, well, heavy.

Mildred automatically pinched the extra flesh at her midriff where it bulged. Midriff bulge had a way of slipping up on one, no matter how many times one declined a spoonful of sugar. Yes, Mildred Budge was dully aware of midriff bulge; but she had, without ever having any proof at all, believed herself smaller and more able to deal with fallen tree limbs than Mrs. Henderson.

Mildred's stomach growled, and she glanced at the clock. She had not finished praying. Her coffee was cold. And she was supposed to teach Sunday school this week. One had to be prayed up to do that. One simply did not dare to rise in the Berean Sunday school class and give voice to scripture without being fully fessed up on one's sins. She glanced at her open Bible impatiently. Mildred had just reached that critical moment in her prayer time when she was about to ask, "Of what do I need to repent, dear Jesus?" when the phone rang.

As Mrs. Henderson began to expound on the dead tree and its hanging limbs, Mildred's concentration split. *What are my sins?* Mildred couldn't think of anything, and that was a bad sign. A very bad sign. No immediate answer meant that Mildred was so far gone, so calloused and unfeeling, that she had lost touch with the reality of God's presence, which she might have gotten closer to if this lonely old woman with a growing cataract and a dead pine tree didn't keep dialing her phone number before eight o'clock in the morning.

It was her fault for picking up that phone. But Mildred simply couldn't help herself. She had tried not picking up before, and Mrs. Henderson had grown frantic and hit the redial button several times until Mildred had finally answered. Then, Mrs. Henderson had gushed, "Oh, my dear, I was about to send the paramedics. I imagined you lying on the floor helpless and hurt and alone."

It was very hard not to answer a ringing telephone if the person on the other end might send the paramedics to the house of the other woman whom she hadn't even called. It was, in short, unconscionable not to answer a wrong number like that.

"Well, it's been grand talking to you," Mrs. Henderson said suddenly. "I'm glad you're doing so well. I was just thinking about you, but I must call my other friend now," Mrs. Henderson said.

Then, just as she heard the line disconnect, Mildred realized that Mrs. Henderson had not misdialed at all. Having learned Mildred Budge's phone number, Mrs. Henderson now included Mildred on her list of single women she checked on.

I am one of them now, Mildred thought—one of the lone women that other people feel that they must check on out of Samaritan kindness.

It was humiliating; it was gratifying.

It was jarring; it was touching.

It was intrusive; it was loving.

The kindness hit Mildred, as well as the bleakness of that position. Her stomach growled again, and she saw her Bible, old friend, waiting to read her. She didn't just read the Bible; it read her.

In an effort to move back into that interior place of prayer, Mildred began to recite scripture to herself: "Though I speak with the tongues of men and of angels, but have not love, I have become as sounding brass or a clanging cymbal. And though I have the gift of prophecy, and understand all mysteries and all knowledge, and though I have all faith, so that I could remove mountains, but have not love, I am nothing."

The words did their work. Mildred forgot that her coffee was cold—and that there was more in the kitchen and it was still hot. She didn't care that she was hungry. Mildred picked up her Bible again with hope and trembling, and finally, the confession of repentance that she needed to make, and which would last through the breakfast hour, began quite simply, "Jesus, I am so sorry I ever thought Mrs. Henderson was fat."

Loading an
Imprecatory Prayer

"I have decided to declare an imprecatory prayer against the hiring of consultants to organize the capital steward-ship campaign," Fran announced, apropos of nothing.

That did not matter. Mildred Budge had been expecting some kind of announcement about trying out an imprecatory prayer ever since the preacher had expounded upon the need for them occasionally, when he preached from the Psalms. It was not about revenge. Christians don't get revenge, but they have a responsi-bility to pray justice into reality, he had said—or some-thing like that.

Sermons didn't remain verbatim in Miss Budge's memory, unless they were direct quotations from the Bible.

Ideas from the preacher were meditated upon and contemplated, even when he tried to compare some aspect of God's will to a big football game or a soccer match. A retired school teacher of fifth grade students, Miss Budge had an affectionate regard for how people of all ages tried to communicate what they meant, and she had long ago adjusted herself to listening to men who liked sports analogies. Last Sunday, the preacher had announced there would be a new capital fund-raising campaign that would begin after the first of the year, and the effort was going to require every member of the team.

"No one can sit this one out on the bench. We will need two hundred volunteers," he said, and the words were more than an announcement; they were kind of a warning, and Mildred had recalled feeling an assault that didn't fit inside a church where one had to learn through the years how to go into laying down one's self-defenses in order to be vulnerable enough and trusting enough for the work of the Holy Spirit. Free will was quite a gift, but it tended to result in willfulness, and one had to learn to lay it down.

Mildred had tried to lay it down the week the preacher had announced the coming campaign, but she had braced against it—had been getting ready, thinking about how much more money she could give to the building campaign, but Fran was doing more.

Though Mildred understood that there were different fruits of the Spirit, different gifts by the Spirit, her friend Fran was more of a doer of the Word. Today, Fran had decided to obey the preacher by proclaiming an imprecatory prayer against—and this was a surprise!— the administrative body of the church that was launching this new campaign announced by the preacher himself.

"What will this prayer be like?" Mildred asked softly, for the answer was private and, although the two women were friends, one still respected the privacy of the other. Prayer could be public, but some were meant to be private. Intensely so.

Fran did not seem to share Mildred's concerns. She leaned her head back, flicking the underside of her jaw the way her husband Gritz used to, strumming her skin with nails that she kept manicured prettily. They were nice hands, well tended, more feminine than Mildred's workhorse hands that looked fine but were rarely polished. Lacquer chipped, and the retired school teacher didn't have time, she said, to replace colored nail polish on a regular basis. No, Sally Hansen's blush-tinted nail gloss was sufficient. When it chipped, the light landed on it in various ways and one could barely tell that the wearer had a tolerance for imperfection. Sometimes Mildred Budge meditated on that, wondering if she had an unhealthy tolerance for sin. Her imperfectly manicured hands suggested as much.

"I'm using David's encounter with Goliath to inspire my prayer," Fran explained, fingernails flicking.

No double chin there.

Mildred pinched the little loose skin under her own chin and grieved.

"Because Goliath represents the world," Mildred deduced, and she thought one more time, *Fran is so good at this praying business.*

"Exactly," Fran said. "Goliath taunted King Saul, and David couldn't stand to have the honor of his king insulted."

Mildred understood immediately, but she did not elaborate for her friend. Mildred had her own gifts, and a willingness to be silent was one of them. Fran needed to say what she thought out loud, and because they were members of a church, where women were expected to keep silent, it was only among women that they could express an opinion that was likely to be unpopular. Say it to a man and you earned yourself a formal rebuke, or worse, a withdrawal of affection. The eyes of an elder could glow warmly when he greeted you on Sunday morning or grow hard and cold if he thought you were a troublemaker; women who had opinions that differed from the leadership of the church were considered troublemakers. Mildred had felt the coldness more than once—been stoned by cold eyes that did not glow warmly inside a morning greeting.

"Using money from tithes to hire a consulting firm to come in and organize a strategy that will manipulate the members of the church to give is an insult to the honor and power of the Holy Spirit, whose work it is to be our boss," Fran said without equivocation, and her intelligent blue eyes narrowed. For in spite of the many years that she had been a widowed homebody, Fran thought like a businessperson but prayed like a church woman.

"Inside and outside the church, I don't like being manipulated," Mildred confessed softly. It was a difficult confession to make, for Christians are disciplined in being used and accept it as part of taking up their crosses.

Neither woman had to say to the other that being manipulated—corralled like a mindless sheep rather than respected as a thinking person whose free will had been bought and protected by Christ on the cross—was disrespectful of God and an abuse of power. It was also a form of faithlessness; when you hire consultants, you say that your own leadership under the authority of the Holy Spirit is not enough to please God, and there is the unmistakable suggestion and worry that the Holy Spirit is absent in the whole process.

But the Holy Spirit wasn't absent. He had led the preacher to preach about imprecatory prayers, and he had led Fran Applewhite to plan an imprecatory prayer about the decision of the administrators to hire consultants to manipulate the congregation into making financial pledges.

No, the Holy Spirit had not receded. He was moving in a mysterious way.

"I am going to pray that the administrators reconsider. Possibly repent," Fran decided aloud.

"Do you need some help from me?" Mildred asked. "You know, where two are gathered—"

Fran shook her head no before Mildred could finish her offer. "David didn't need anybody. One slingshot, one stone."

"A one-woman job," Mildred agreed.

Fran nodded decisively. "One imprecatory prayer, and I'm going to speak it."

Vows and Codicils

When the minister asked whether the congregation would agree to help raise the newly baptized child, he looked about expectantly to see the raised right hands of the congregation as a whole in signaling a vow before God that they were willing.

Mildred Budge kept her hands tightly clasped in her lap, as usual, for she did not make vows lightly. Because she did not know the couple or the child, she did not see how she could authentically vow to help raise a child she didn't know. Mildred Budge did not make vows to God just to be polite.

But in following the gaze of the minister, Mildred saw her best friend Fran quickly signal with a raised hand that she, too, would participate in this vow of shared parenthood within the church.

Fran's response was so contrary to their on-going discussions about when to make a vow to God that Mildred could barely concentrate during the prayer time following the baptism.

After service, in the car on the way to a preacher-forbidden lunch at the country club, Mildred asked Fran, "Did I see your hand move in a vow to God that you would help raise the baby?"

"Sort of," Fran replied easily, finding a parking spot. "It was really more of a wave, kind of like saying, 'I'm here if you need me.' Like that," she affirmed comfortably.

Pulling at the backs of their skirts, the two long-time friends click-clacked their way across the asphalt parking lot toward the deluxe lunch buffet, as Fran explained, "Sometimes I get tired of not raising my hand."

"I just don't see how we can be expected to make a vow we can't envision keeping." Mildred replied, repeating herself.

Mildred had said the words before. Fran had heard the argument before. There were, indeed, times when Mildred and Fran had conversations so familiar that they didn't even need to say them out loud again. They had both made individual vows to God that they had been keeping. Fran was careful to explain in the report of her vows to her best friend that there was a codicil.

"I promised God that I would give up strawberries except when Dinzel's had them dipped in chocolate during the spring." Fran had made the vow after a severe hiatal hernia attack that she blamed on the seeds in the strawberries she had just eaten. It was a reasonable codicil to a vow that, if God would rescue her from her present distress, she would not put the vessel of the Lord in jeopardy again—except during an extraordinary season, such as the chocolate-covered strawberry season.

Mildred's most regretted vow—and there were no codicils—had involved a misadventure twenty years ago with a contact lens that got stuck underneath a recalcitrant eye lid. Since then, she had worn only glasses. She had kept her vow that, if God would remove that contact lens from deep underneath her eyelid, she wouldn't wear them again; but since that time, someone had invented tinted contact lenses. Occasionally, Mildred wondered what it would be like to have blue eyes instead of brown. Her vow kept her from finding out.

Neither woman told either of those stories of vows to God, but they hummed inside each woman as their conversation continued.

"Our objection to vowing to help parents raise their children is based on not teaching Sunday school anymore. It is simply a vow we cannot reasonably keep," Mildred reminded Fran.

"We could pray. That counts," Fran suggested thoughtfully. Then Fran cut her eyes at Mildred, realizing that each of them had a prayer list so long already that adding another item to it seemed an occupation that neither of them would be prepared to maintain. They both had already wrestled with the concept of good works appointed for her. Each woman knew that there was a distinct difference between being agreeable to doing the works expected by God and doing the busy work assigned by administrators within the church whose job review depended to some extent on their ability to recruit and manage volunteer labor.

A church lady's work was potentially less problematic in its way. Guided and guarded by a division of labor based on gender, a church lady had many safety nets for saying no and yes to what was asked of her. Fran and Mildred had decided that not vowing to raise other people's children was right, based on the truth that teaching Sunday school was a stage in their lives they had left behind.

Walking down the lunch table buffet, as they fixed their plates, Fran popped a piece of fried okra into her mouth and nodded approvingly to Mildred, who spooned some onto her plate, next to the glorious turkey and dressing that was also unexpectedly there.

They sat down at their reserved table, bowing their heads for a blessing that was so deep, so internal, so eternal, that both women raised their heads at the same time, saying, "Amen," simultaneously as they picked up their respective forks.

"So, what made you raise your hand today?" Mildred pressed.

Fran tasted the cornbread dressing, closing her eyes briefly in approval, savoring the sage, and then meditatively replied, "Don't you ever get tired of saying no to what you have decided isn't your good work to do?"

Mildred nodded her head readily, tasting the turkey. "Yes. There are times when I would like to say yes to everything they ask of me, from mission trips to playing the organ for choir rehearsal."

"You don't know how to play the organ," Fran said.

"True. But if I did, I'd say yes, except for funerals. I don't want to play the organ at funerals. That is actually why I've never learned to play the organ," Mildred explained, tipping some cranberry sauce near her dressing to complete the perfection of the next bite.

"So here we are—two veteran church ladies— who have learned how to say no with aplomb, guilt-lessly, and we now want to say yes to everything," Fran summed.

"They don't teach you about that in Sunday school," Mildred replied.

Fran shook her head solemnly. "No, they don't prepare you in Sunday school for all of the ways you want to say yes to show how much you love other people and God."

Mildred nodded as a skilled waiter placed a silver saucer of warm buttered crackers near her elbow. "See? This is what the preacher doesn't understand. It is very difficult to fast when the Bridegroom is present."

"He would be present in our homes if one of us still cooked," Fran replied tartly, for although each woman had come to terms with eating Sunday lunch out, which caused other people to work on a day appointed for rest, each woman continued to wrestle with the question—and so many others—that was part of working out one's salvation with fear and hope.

"Living with Jesus is so absolutely good," Fran said suddenly, taking a warm saltine. This was, in fact, the second blessing over the meal.

Mildred took one too, nibbling the crisp buttered corner before popping it into her mouth. Delicious. Their conversation that followed was more of the same—words spoken to each other but intended to be overheard as praise and unceasing prayer by the Bridegroom, the hearer of vows and their codicils: the Maker of each day's feast.

Cleaning House

When the Sunday school teacher, who was a retired public school teacher like Mildred, began her morning's lesson with the question "How many of you are living with too much clutter?" there was the predictable laughter that rippled around the room as if to confess, "Oh, yes, I am a sinner."

For there is a time in a mature woman's more seasoned life when she is so accustomed to acknowledging the reality of sin that she readily confesses to almost any type of trespass to keep other sinners company. It is considered polite church-going behavior.

Still, the women sat back a bit more firmly in their metal chairs, planted both feet on the ground, and waited for the next shoe to drop—or rather, the next question that this educator, trained in the Socratic method, asked: "Why do you live with so much clutter? You can't take it with you. Isn't it weighing you down?"

Well, of course it was weighing them all down, Mildred thought, almost irritably, for as much as she enjoyed being with and getting along with her friends at church, sometimes she longed for the opportunity to be at church without feeling condemned over some aspect of her humanity, and she was human after all.

Sure, she needed to clean house.

Sure, she needed to weed out the kitchen catch-all drawer with its collection of rubber bands, loose batteries, twist-ties, and recipes torn raggedly out of the daily newspaper. She had cleaned the drawer out many times before, but it always ended up like it was now: full of stuff that she had to plow through to find what she needed. On the bright side, what she needed was usually there.

Even if that crowded kitchen drawer did not condemn her, there were other pockets of clutter around her house, and Mildred knew right where they were: places in closets where she hadn't vacuumed the floor in a long time because of too many pairs of shoes and the top shelf was overloaded with clothes because it was hard to let go of some garments that, once upon a time, had felt like home against her skin. That red shiny pantsuit didn't fit her anymore, but it used to look great on her—and there was a chance that she might lose twenty pounds and be able to wear it again. To let it go symbolized giving up hope that she would ever lose *that* twenty pounds.

And the sewing box—the one she didn't use for mending clothes—was the one her mother had given her on her sixteenth birthday. It rested on the floor underneath the red shiny pantsuit and was so valuable that Mildred had requested in her will that it be buried with her. The peach-lined sewing box contained artifacts of history so intimate that she had to be at her strongest—and usually holding a glass of champagne on New Year's Eve—to sort through it.

It held her mother's favorite pair of sewing scissors, the measuring gauge her mother had used to teach Mildred how to hem skirts, packets of pins, and spools of thread that once upon a time were the perfect match for garments long since given to the Faith Rescue Mission. When Mildred pulled out a thread now, it usually broke from age. Underneath those aged spools were three different packets of love letters that she hadn't read in years. They made her smile to see them, but she felt no need to read them. She knew exactly what they said.

Sarah leaned forward, arm on the podium, and confessed, "My house is so crowded now that I don't have any room left to store anything else. What can I do?" she asked, and there was a hint of real inquiry in her voice, a kind of beseechment, as if the woman who usually knew the answers to her own questions didn't know the answer to this one.

But it appeared that other women did, for they began to raise their hands and offer house cleaning techniques that were designed to declutter.

First you do this. Then you do that.

Ladies smiled, for they had heard the tips many times and said them often to others, especially young brides who, in the early days of keeping a house, were perplexed: so many wedding gifts and so little space to store them all.

At last, without even a nod to scripture, a woman who rarely spoke raised a gentle hand and reported, "I asked my husband if I were to die would he marry again, and he said that he most likely would. I said, 'Well if you do, are you going to let your new wife wear my clothes?' He said that if they fit, he saw no reason why she shouldn't wear them. I said, 'Are you going to let her have my jewelry, too?' He said, 'Well, you won't be here, and if I love her, I don't see why she shouldn't wear the jewelry that is a symbol of my love.' So I said to him, 'Are you going to let her go through my drawers and closets?' He said, 'Well, if it is her house, I expect she will because women are in charge of the drawers and the closets.'"

The wise woman took a deep breath and let that prophecy take hold. The room was deathly quiet. Then, she added succinctly, "My will is completely up-to-date, with my jewelry going to my daughters, and my house has been decluttered ever since."

The woman who rarely spoke became quiet then, her hands resting in her lap, and Mildred marveled, once again, how wise it is to talk little so that when you do speak people listen carefully. As Mildred looked around the room, she saw wide-eyed women considering who might take their place if they were called to Glory sooner than their husbands, and she saw that even as they considered the state of their closets and drawers, they were also imagining that there were women sitting right there in that room who might become the second wife of their present husbands after their deaths and see inside their closets and drawers.

A restlessness pervaded the room as Sarah finally read the scripture of the day that warned against covetousness. Women who were usually very good at sitting still were like a line of horses at the starting gate waiting for the signal, so that they could run the race set before them. It was a very determined race to go home and clean out closets and drawers and add codicils to wills, appointing which daughter, granddaughter, or niece would inherit which pieces of jewelry, while they cast half-angry, half-disappointed glances at confused husbands, who said to each other later, before the evening service began, "I didn't get a nap today. My old girl came home from Sunday school with a bee in her bonnet about housecleaning, and she had me carrying bags out to the trunk of the car so that I can tote them to the mission tomorrow."

"Me, too," the men said, one after another.

Mildred did not have a husband to help her clean house, but she swooped down upon the kitchen drawer alone and ruthlessly cleaned it out. Like her sisters who were cleaning out their houses, she did feel better, lighter. Then, she turned her attention to the overflowing sewing basket and decided that she could let the spools of old thread go, but that was all. The love letters remained next to her mother's scissors and the hemming gauge. She tossed six pairs of shoes, so she could vacuum thoroughly, and she took away an armful of clothes that no longer fit, except the red pant-suit. She kept that shiny red pantsuit. A woman needed hope and her memories, especially the memory—which wasn't clutter—of how she had looked and felt once upon a time.

Mildred Budge Sows a Wild Oat (or not)

When my friend Mildred Budge feels like sowing a wild oat, she makes a left-hand turn when a right-hand turn would have been a safer choice.

Her most recent veering from the safest path occurred last Sunday when she was asked to lead the morning prayer in Sunday school without any advance notice. She said yes. Then she didn't follow the usual prayer route.

There is an accepted structure in leading the morning prayer in Sunday school. First, you read a selected scripture from the Bible, and if you can't find one that you think fits, you simply quote a psalm.

Mildred didn't do either one. She bowed her head, and the next thing we all knew, she was practically shouting Ezekiel-like images at us instead—something about dry bones coming to life. I was wondering why she didn't choose that sweet verse about having our youth being renewed like an eagle's, instead, when, suddenly, she launched right into a full-blown prayer that 1) did not begin with thanksgiving or a confession of sin, and 2) did not ask for prayer requests from her classmates, which is the time and place when many of us catch up with the week's news!

Honestly, I opened my eyes to see if Mildred Budge was having some kind of fit, and she was standing kind of lopsided-like, slightly pigeon-toed, and with her hands raised to the sky. Nobody does that here, except the preachers, and they only do it on special occasions.

Then, with her beige slip showing a good two inches, Mildred made one left-hand turn after another in her prayer, until she stopped all of a sudden and asked God to help us tell each other the truth when we needed to hear it, and to tell God the truth.

Fear of being seen with my eyes open had caused me to close them again, but I opened them back up when Mildred said that part about telling each other the truth. I saw a lot of women wondering if Mildred had someone in particular in mind that she wanted to rebuke—or was she, bless her heart, confessing to being a sinner in front of God and everyone?

I really felt sorry for her and promised myself that I would not agree to say the morning prayer unless I had some advance notice, because this kind of public breakdown could happen to anyone.

The end result was that poor Mildred looked like an ordinary sinner and, basically, dared every other church woman in Sunday school to tell her what was wrong with her.

No one said amen afterward.

We were all afraid to and never more glad to turn in our Bibles to the lesson for the day, which was unfortunately on a similar topic: the speck/plank injunction, wherein we were reminded not to point out other people's speck-sized sins until we dealt with the plank-sized ones in our own lives.

Poor Mildred Budge. She looked guilty as sin, and sin can be such a sore subject. We were reminded of the nature of sin during the Sunday school hour, to the point that we raced each other out the door when it was over. Afterward, I lingered during the coffee break before service began to see what the other gals were saying. No one was talking about Millie Budge, which was logical, because I am her third best friend after Fran and Belle; if the gals were going to talk about Millie, they wouldn't do it in front of me or them.

I caught up with Mildred in church on our regular pew, and we listened to the young boy preacher who sometimes fills in for our minister when he's away preaching at a missions conference. The boy preached the gospel today as if no one had ever heard it before.

Then the very young man led us in a corporate confession of sin, which we all said together. I listened to Mildred beside me, and she got through it just fine—didn't even stumble a bit, which surprised me.

Later, in her car, when we were making a completely unnecessary left-hand turn because it is entirely possible to get to Sunday lunch at our country club by just making one right-handed turn after another, I asked her point blank: "What got into you this morning, Mildred?"

Budge acted like she didn't know what I was talking about, so I reminded her that she had prayed we would tell the truth to each other, and so I just had to ask her, "Why would you choose Sunday school to sow a wild oat?"

She cocked her head and replied thoughtfully, "I thought I was sowing seeds of righteousness."

"It looked like a wild oat to me," I replied truthfully, because she's the one who prayed that we would tell her the truth.

And then Mildred Budge looked at me oddly, as if we hadn't known each other thirty years, and said, "Sometimes it is hard to tell, isn't it?"

Lessons in Picking Up a Man At Church

When the old man's walker caught on the green shag carpet and flipped sideways, leaving him to totter dangerously unaided in his pilgrimage to his favorite pew on Sunday morning, stout Mildred Budge reacted. She saw that her old friend was about to fall, smack his jaw against the wooden pew, bounce off of that, land badly on the floor, break his hip, and end up in the nursing home again, where he would die of an infection this time. So, naturally, Miss Budge leapt to her feet with arms outstretched and caught Mr. Johnson securely under the armpits. Then she shifted her right arm to embrace him and used the other to scoop him up the way a groom traditionally lifts a bride, only she was a sixtyish woman who, in the moment of that adrenaline rush, had superhuman strength. (She had been strong her whole life but had learned to hide it, the way she had worked hard to keep her gift with numbers a secret, too.)

The members of the congregation, who were already in their respective places, collectively froze, immobilized by the image of an older lady of the church picking up an elder emeritus and depositing him safely on his pew. She then had the indelicacy to grunt. Church-lady sounds included laughing generously at the right time, tsk-tsk-tsking at other right times, sighing sadly at the right times, and, when they were on the verge of being exposed as people who knew how to live wisely, they hid their light under a bushel by dithering, which was accompanied by a fluttering of their hands next to their faces, as if to fan away the very idea that they knew much of anything. These sounds came easily to Mildred Budge, but she used them all sparingly, for she embraced the silence assigned to women, not because she was absolutely convinced that shushing women was theologically undeniable (How could you praise God and be quiet too?), but because she thought people talked too much, and telling one gender to be quiet was an efficient way to keep the hub-bub down. For these and other reasons, she was schooled in the discipline of keeping silent and keeping her own counsel. But Miss Budge was also given to being hospitable, and so she made the church-lady sounds when they were called for, fluttered her hands when paid a compliment, but she never, ever grunted publicly, until the morning she picked up Mr. Johnson.

The sound echoed, condemning her for her indelicacy and for being stronger than a woman was expected to be. Being strong surprised others. It had surprised Mildred, too, but she was learning how to embrace her strengths because she needed them. In spite of the many times that the church had launched and relaunched the shepherding system, moving elders and deacons around to try and make meaningful matches between helpers of the church and people in the church who needed help, Miss Budge had never had a shepherd who had ever come to her home to change a lightbulb for her. That would have been nice—having a shepherd who would climb a ladder and take out a bulb and put a new one in, but that hope had never been realized. The failure was understandable, for even as women had their own pressures to manage, men in the church did too. Assigned to single women who needed help, men were simultaneously warned not to be alone with single women, since it could lead to moral failure. How could you change a single woman's lightbulb and not endanger yourself and her, too? Yes, Mildred Budge understood why the shepherd system failed: helping a single lady could lead to the commission of sin, and not helping her was, at its worst, only the sin of omission. The consequences of the lesser evil were easier to bear. And besides, somehow single ladies' lightbulbs got changed after all.

And so, Miss Budge continued to climb her own ladder when necessary, change her own lightbulbs, mow her own front yard, and tote bags of canned goods to various food banks year round. She had learned over and over again that she was not only simply strong, she was incredibly strong, having inherited her daddy's muscle tone, though her muscles were hidden under the fleshy appearance of a woman who enjoyed her food. Famous for her potluck dish of family-size cherry cobblers for church fellowship suppers, she had never exercised her other considerable strengths in enterprises that might have resulted in a leaner shape, which would have tele-graphed to others, who knew her before it happened dramatically that Sunday morning, that she—a church lady in good standing—was strong enough to pick up a falling man at church.

So it came as a surprise to everyone when she did.

Miss Budge could feel the eyes of others upon her as she backed away from Mr. Johnson, whose head was lowered, for it was a shame to be picked up by a woman, a shame for a man to be weak, even when he was ninety-ish, a shame to need help, whether you were a man or a woman, even if you went to a church where the gospel of Good Samaritanism was taught and where one lesson after another urged the members of the flock to bear one another's burdens. It didn't say, "Never, under any circumstances, should a woman of the church pick up a man."

But that happened to Mildred Budge and to Mr. Johnson, and the crowd of witnesses were members of their church who, out of respect for the two of them, caught in their exposed positions of strong and weak, hastily opened Bibles to meditate upon the scripture highlighted in the church bulletin, as the day's mes-sage, and upon which the preacher would expound shortly. The flock also prayed, sending up silent prayers of intercession on behalf of Mildred Budge, not sure exactly why they were fearful for her and her reputation, but aware, in some unnamed way that, although she had not sinned, exactly, she had broken one of the unspoken and unwritten commandments about what was expected of women in church.

They prayed next for Mr. Johnson, a widower, and when they did, their minds ruminated about how long he had been a widower and whether the thirty-year age difference was too great an impediment for him and Mildred to live happily ever after. But, really, she had never married, and Mr. Johnson could solve that problem. And she could solve his. He obviously needed a caregiver, and she was suited for that task—she could lift him and everything!—and it was in that way that the event was digested and Miss Budge's place and Mr. Johnson's place in the congregation reassigned and also reimagined. There were glints of knowing in the eyes of others that something acceptable, like a romance, was possible between the two dears now, and the idea covered a multitude—well, it wasn't a multitude of sins, exactly—it was just that one dreadful misstep that occurred, not just when Mr. Johnson tripped, but when Mildred Budge, in front of God and everyone, had forgotten who she was supposed to be and how she was supposed to act, and had picked up a man at church.

The Artist and Mildred Budge

I only asked her to pose naked for me to rattle her. She was one of those staid, self-satisfied church ladies who go through life holding onto Jesus the way they clutch their purses against their sides with the handle captured securely in the crook of their aging elbows. Like other tourists, these women come through my gallery, looking at my pictures, as if they know what art is. I watch the way they look at my work, but they don't pay any attention to how I look at them—as if the way I see doesn't matter, and it's everything. I see, therefore, I am. I am an artist.

I see the skin that is rough at their elbows, the way it is on their heels no matter how many pedicures they get. They walk around secure, like they know everything important, but they don't know that there are some things, like dry skin, they don't have to put up with. Has something to do with not being vain. They are not supposed to be vain—it's one of their rules from the Bible.

Because they read the Bible, they put up with decline, deterioration, middle-age spread that does something worse in their eighties, and they appear not to hear the jokes made at their expense. (Maybe they're deaf, but I don't think so. I think they hear a lot and just don't react.) That was one of my theories I decided to test the day this Southern church lady came into my art gallery and walked around looking at my pictures, hard, like she knew what art is.

I snuck up on her, expecting her to jump when I asked her a question, but she didn't. "Are you here for long?" I asked.

"Three days," she said, turning slowly, as if she didn't want to stop looking at my work, which made me feel a little jumpy.

I didn't like how she was looking at my work, as if she could see my art the way I saw the subjects I painted. I looked at her, hard, the way she was looking at my work, even though I figured I would not make a sale this way. Church ladies don't usually buy my work, except if it is a picture of a live oak tree. They love trees, and live oaks are the main tree around here. Fairhope, Alabama, is right on the Gulf of Mexico.

When I thought about it, she kind of reminded me of a live oak, really, the way she was standing, feet apart, toes pointed in opposite directions, the weight of her aged self balanced perfectly, and her gaze the kind that reminds me of the horizon when the sun is setting over the water. I both admired and hated her for the way she stood there.

Her brown eyes kinda smiled, and when her gaze connected with mine beside a series of three nudes, she said, "Who is the lovely girl?"

I said, "She doesn't want people to know who she is, but I can tell you she's a social worker."

We looked together at the three nudes, and I couldn't remember the model's name, so I said, "It's amazing the conversations you have with a model when she's nude. It's a very intense situation. Secrets get told. The truth gets told."

The woman nodded as if she understood that, and she couldn't possibly, so I asked, "You appreciate art?"

She shrugged gently, and for the life of me, I don't know what that shrug was supposed to be: you either do or you don't appreciate art, so why not a yes or no? So I figured I would see if she could make a decision that required one of those words. I said, "There's something about you I'd like to paint. Would you pose nude for me?"

The question should have sent her running from the shop. Instead, a smile dawned upon her face—yes, dawned, like the sun coming up. It worked its way across the horizon of her face, moving the corners of her mouth, bringing forth light from eyes that had at first seemed brown but which became golden with her smile. As I watched, my hand itched for a sketch pad, while that part of my brain that sorts out the best medium for different subjects rejected charcoal (too messy), pastels (too soft), pen and ink (not enough shading), and finally, oils, only I wasn't sure really if oils could do her justice if I were to paint her. Even as I calculated that, I didn't want to try and paint her, for I thought I would surely fail, and perhaps it was that inner acknowledgement that I would fail—live oaks are very hard to paint, for though they give the appearance of stillness, they are actually alive, and this woman was beginning to remind me more of a live oak than the horizon, now that I was really looking at her—that caused me to ask her to pose nude for me.

She should have made a dash out the front door, but she didn't. Instead, she began to look at me, as if I were one of my own paintings, and said, "My dear, I am of an age when only my doctor sees me in a state of undress, and that only when I feel the encounter is unavoidable."

It took me a couple of seconds to translate what she meant, and something inside of me that felt mean grew intense; inexplicably, I hated her, but that fire still caused me to want to draw her.

"Nudity is a state of mind," I replied airily, shifting so she could freely leave my gallery.

She didn't. "It is quite an adventurous idea to be carefully observed by someone who can see what you see," she announced after a long pause.

Her voice stopped being music and became the voice that models who have posed nude for me before have often used, for it is absolutely true that a model and an artist experience a deep intimacy of confession. The artist tells the model truths not revealed except through the work, and the model, with nothing left to hide, often spills secrets so deeply kept and previously held so close that, after a series of posing sessions, the model appears to not only be nude but to have shed weight physically and spiritually.

I have seen this happen, but I cannot prove it.

And then she pivoted slowly, looking carefully—almost reverentially—at my work, and I felt exposed and inexplicably nervous.

When she finished her rotation, she cocked her head at me, appeared to hear something I couldn't hear, and said, "How long would you need me to sit for you?"

I was so taken aback by her willingness to pose nude that, at first, I couldn't answer.

As her gaze searched my mind for clues about why I had asked her (as if she could determine the nature of my artistic vision—the audacity of that! Really!), I decided to call her bluff. *Don't play chicken with me. I can last longer.* "We could start now, if you are free, and then, if it goes well, a couple of hours tomorrow. You would need to be fully naked," I said for emphasis.

She nodded and shifted to look behind herself at the series of nudes. "That girl was older than you drew her," she calculated. "Do you plan to change my age?"

I looked at my own work again. I had *youthened* the portraits. It was true. I recalled erasing a line or two—that's all it takes to make a woman's face younger. And I remembered making her younger because, when I looked in her eyes, there was more suffering than I had expected, and I erased some of that too.

"Social workers see so much," the woman observed as her purse slid down her arm and began to swing at her side. "Who would greet the customers?" she asked suddenly. "If you and I are working in your studio?"

"I will close the gallery," I said with a shrug, though I did not want to close up my shop. Like artists everywhere, I needed to make every sale I could. Still, it was a game of chicken, and I wouldn't lose—no way this woman wearing stockings in the heat of the day would take them off because a stranger asked her to.

"Where is your studio?" she asked.

"There," I replied, pointing behind her to the area where my easel stood on display.

People like to see an easel in an artist's gallery. They think it proves the place belongs to an artist, though if I had been asked, I would have said that the colored tile of the flooring that supported the easel was greater proof that I am who I say I am: it's beautiful. I bought the tile from the Robert F. Henry Tile Company, and it's mottled with earth tones. The Robert F. Henry Tile Company is as famous for its tile as this city is famous for its live oak trees and the view of the gulf.

People come here year round for the water and the live oaks and the small-town shopping and to ramble through artists' galleries, like mine.

We all play the parts assigned to us by the people who market our small city as a tourist destination. Even the name is a marketer's dream: Fairhope.

"Would I sit or stand?" she asked, looking past my easel and to the tile floor. She walked to it and her posture changed. She laid down her purse beside the easel, and took off her shoes.

That wasn't right. Even models who have done this before expect a robe and a screen. They take their clothes off in private, put on the robe, come back out, take the robe off, and after a minute of nervous fidgeting and the awkward jokes told when one person is naked and the other is not, the work begins.

It is glorious work. It is my work. And it still takes my breath away that I am the one who is supposed to do it. I am supposed to see and tell beauty to the world. It is hard work. It is my work. I am an artist. Only I see what I see. Only I can express what my eyes see.

"I can give you an hour right now," the church lady announced evenly.

Then, she did the most remarkable thing. She took off her glasses, looked at me for directions of where to put them, and I, still playing what I was calling a game of chicken, pointed to a small chair where children sit sometimes when they get bored with their parents who complete deals with me. She walked to the chair, sat down, set her shoes to the side, and laid her glasses on the small table beside the chair.

She was waiting for me to do something, and I realized that she expected me to close my shop.

Shaking my head in amazement, I walked over to the front door, flipped over the side of the sign that announced that I was gone to lunch, and twisted the lock. I closed the blinds.

By the time I returned, she had taken off her navy skirt and jacket and was standing there in one of those old-fashioned white slips with a bit of lace on it, and she was beautiful. I almost said, "That's fine right there. Don't change a thing. You are perfect just like that."

But then she would have won, and I didn't really want to tell her she was beautiful, although I imagine she had not heard that much in her life.

I switched out the canvas, grabbed my pencil, and answered her earlier question. "Would you stand? Can you stand—the way you were standing before with your toes out, perfectly balanced?"

"Without my clothes?" she confirmed.

"Nude," I confirmed. I don't like to lose.

She readily undressed and, as she did, I knew that I was the only person who had asked her to take her clothes off in years, and the way she did it belied the truth: she was a deeply modest person.

I wondered why she was willing to expose herself so readily to someone like me—a character playing the part of an artist in a shop on Main Street in Fairhope, Alabama, but I would not be able to find the answer to that question absolutely. Inexplicably, as soon as she had undressed, I felt that familiar ignition of vision and a yearning to tell it; and so before I could actually make the kind of joke that is meant to put a model at ease, I found myself inside the activity of telling her story instead, on the canvas, and it was such a story that I couldn't stop to make small talk.

She was only naked for an instant, and then she wasn't naked the way people think of being nude any longer. Her body was undressed, but there was something else that clothed her, and I guess it was dignity, for there was no shame in her exposure, and I got over being nervous right away.

I immediately entered that zone where artists go to do their work. Like the most seasoned models, she entered the silence immediately with me and did not interrupt my vision or my concentration, and I did not even have to be grateful. When I suddenly came out of my world to realize that she was tired, I felt the sweat pouring from my face and the familiar painful strain between my shoulders, for beauty demands quite a lot of you. When I asked her if she, too, was suffering from standing on her feet, she smiled benignly, the way people dismiss the idea that they could be hungry after missing lunch.

With that idea, I recalled that, upon initially seeing her, I had thought she was one of those old-fashioned church-going women and scanned her neck, but no traditional cross hung on a gold chain there, though it seemed to me that it once had, which is the kind of thought that artists have: we can see what once was or could be.

To confirm that I was right, I said, "You're a Christian."

As she began to get dressed, I turned away, for it is one thing to look at a model with the eyes of an artist, but quite another to be a peeping Tom. She dressed easily with her back turned to me, and I marveled that she had not said much, since church women usually rattle on; so I repeated my claim: "You're a Christian."

"I believe so," she agreed, as the slip came down over her head, and I thought her movements, seen peripherally, were graceful and that she was limber and easy with herself in a way that belied her seasoned age and the types of clothes she wore, which looked to me, still, like more of a uniform than a skirt and blouse and low-heeled shoes.

I sat down, once the stockings and slip were back on, my eyes moving to the street, because someone came up to the door and peered into my shop intently, and I consider that rude, rude, rude. If the sign on the door says I'm closed, I'm closed, dammit. I looked around at my paintings on the wall and wanted to take them down, and stack them all up and put them where the prying eyes of people on the street who think that I am a retailer could not see them.

But then she wouldn't have seen them.

And she had seen them.

And now she was looking at me, and her face was different, the way the gulf waters change as the light of the day shifts. Now she was younger than she had been when she first arrived, and while I was tired, she appeared to have taken a nap. Her complexion had grown softer, and there was a rosy hue to her cheeks, and the hair on her head had curled a bit more, framing her face. She looked younger, and I thought that I could paint her for years and most likely never capture what was happening inside of her. Live beauty. She was alive like the live oaks are. She pulsed with life—a different pulsing than human movement. She was pure energy, and it had a name but I didn't know it.

Her eyes found me; for an instant, I was lost inside her golden-brown gaze that beamed with that energy. "Do you need me to come back tomorrow?" she asked, picking up her handbag. Her voice was small, childlike now, and I couldn't tell if she wanted to get out of coming back tomorrow—or if she really would come back.

"Would you?" I asked, as we walked slowly past my work to the door.

"If you need me to," she replied placidly. "Do you need me to?"

The game stopped then. Truth won. "I will never be able to finish a picture of you," I admitted.

"That is true," she replied, waiting for me to unlock the door. "You're quite a good artist to be able to see that," she said.

And then we had the conversation that artists and models usually have during the session. It happened on the threshold of my studio, standing on the earthen art of the Robert F. Henry Tile Company.

"Why did you say yes? You really shouldn't have said yes," I explained.

"There was nothing wrong with saying yes to you. You are an artist," she said simply.

Her words slayed me. I know that I am an artist, but it is quite another thing to have someone else know it.

"How would you know anything at all about what an artist is or needs or does?" I asked, and tears welled up in me that hadn't been close to the surface in years. I made them stop.

"I wouldn't, ordinarily," she agreed, and her head began to move gently, as if it were floating on her body. She was thinking. Listening. Seeking and finding words.

I loved her then. Loved her instantly, wanted to claim her as mine somehow—a relative, at least.

"You're a Christian," I repeated. "I've never really understood how people could be Christians. It's rather old-fashioned now. And Jesus—well, Jesus is a joke, a message on a bumper sticker. A cliché in the mouths of televangelists."

"I will not disagree with you," she replied easily, and she reached out and put her hand on my forearm: the one I use to hold my tools to tell the story of what I see, which is how I was born. I was comforted by her touch, as comforted as I was made uncomfortable earlier when she had really seen my work through her eyes that were schooled in finding truth. Really seen it the way I wanted others to see it. Only she, a Christian, had seen my work. And me.

"You're very brave, you know. Very brave. Jesus knows that about you, and because I am a Christian, I do, too."

I waved away the name of Jesus, and even though I loved her hand on my arm, I stepped back from it. I loved her and wanted to hit her at the same time, for if Jesus was real, then he had made me an artist, and it is not easy to be an artist: it is hard work to see what others can't and tell that by yourself.

As if reading my mind, she said, "Jesus sees what you see and he understands," she said as her hand fell to her side, and the floating movement of her head changed to a series of small nods, as if she was agreeing with herself because she didn't think I would.

We were at that place then—where I needed to be grateful. She had done me a favor, and I was supposed to let her testify, which is what Christians do. I figured then that she had stripped naked so that she would have the right to dump salvation on me, but I've heard it all before, and I don't believe in Jesus, and I don't usually like the people who do. I am an artist, and if Jesus is real, he, more than anybody, would understand that I don't live on clichés. I can't recite them, like those verses from the Bible that people use to brainwash themselves into feeling as if they are a part of the club of people who believe that they are fearfully and wonderfully made. Snowflakes, all.

I would have said all of that to the church lady, if she hadn't been such a kid inside that older lady's body, but she was a kid standing there, almost pigeon-toed (okay, I got that wrong: it looked like she was well-balanced) but she was only a kid, and like a kid, she was saying that Jesus was real, and she had said that Jesus thinks I'm brave.

As soon as I felt those words again, I didn't feel brave. Some days, I don't even feel like I can go on, can't even open the shop or welcome strangers to look at the most precious parts of myself hanging naked and exposed on the walls, where numbers that constitute a price telegraph wrongly that what I see and do is up for sale. Has a price. A price! Who can possibly understand that beauty has no price?

She inhaled as I thought those words, and even though I had pulled back from her, she reached out with her fingertips this time and touched the back of my fingers, as if I were a violin and she was testing the strings to see what sound I would make. A pain inside of me that I had learned to live with and ignore surged to the front of my consciousness, and I determined that, as soon as she was gone, I would take three Ibuprofens, not open the shop, but go lie down. I was so tired. Really tired.

"Jesus loves you—this I know," she said softly, and I thought for an instant that she was about to sing a lullaby, and I wanted to hear it and fall asleep believing it. What would that be like? To sleep believing that?

"For the Bible tells you so," I said, finished the child's lyric for her from a deep and foreign place inside myself, where memory kept hold of the songs that we are taught when we don't know that we will hold the words for our whole lives.

"Ask God to help you. He will," she replied simply. She reached past me and twisted the lock, then the doorknob, and with her white slip hanging a little longer than her navy skirt, the lace dancing, sort of, she went back onto Main Street and into the sunlight.

Her absence left a coldness behind and a loneliness that I couldn't name, and I heard myself moan, "Jesus, you've got your nerve," as if he really existed.

I took several deep breaths and then stepped out onto the sidewalk and saw the town of Fairhope as tourists like to find it, with the shopkeepers bustling and the visitors better dressed than the ones at an amusement park, moving at the pace of the waves that come in softly here, unless there's a hurricane, and she wasn't there. I couldn't see her. But she had been in my shop. I had met her and seen her, and my story of her was on the easel: my partial portrait told the unfinished story of a life that wasn't still—one that couldn't be told because her life would never be over. I saw that much, and I wondered what her name was and if I would see her again.

Coming soon: *Cloverdale*—a novel that explores identity, featuring Mildred Budge and her Berean friends.

Acknowledgments

The Berean Sunday school class inspires many people, and I am one of them. I thank particularly leaders in our class who set such wonderful examples of hospitality and wisdom: Kathleen Hutchison, who knows Jesus and knows how to teach Sunday school; Dr. Sarah Portis, who challenges the class to declutter our lives regularly; and Lulie Grant, the loveliest woman you could ever hope to meet and who keeps us focused on grace with grace.

In addition to my Sunday school class, I have found inspiration for the Mildred Budge stories with my lunch bunch, a group of Southern women who meet for Sunday lunch, occasionally, to count their blessings. I have shared some good meals and even more nourishing conversations with Marjorie Dubina, who does believe in "getting real"; Anne Richardson, who embodies goodness; Hazel Quiggins, a genuine Southern raconteur who makes us all laugh; Marjorie Callander, a wry commentator on life in the South, and Bonnie Shanahan, who reminds me of a Southern garden filled with magnolias.

Other friends who inspire Mildred's adventures are Lori Tennimon, who insists on living truthfully; Sue Luckey, a beautiful human being who never misses a chance to encourage someone; and the practically perfect Jennie Polk, who is now a practically perfect grandmother. I am also grateful for the friendship of their husbands: Dan Tennimon, Ron Luckey and Bill Polk.

A special thank you also to my long-time colleague at Auburn University Montgomery, Dr. Alan Gribben, an esteemed Mark Twain scholar, who has generously encouraged my writing by simply helping me to stay employed at the university where we both work. Thank you, Alan.

I also thank my niece, Katie Simpkins DeBortoli, for drawing the picture I needed of Carol Henry, an artist in her own right and the model who inspired the image of Mildred Budge. And I thank my sisters Julie Helms, Patty DeBortoli and Mary Ellen McCord for their faithful love and encouragement.

As usual, I send my love and gratitude to Jack Cates of Cates Optical, a man who helps me to see Jesus better—and everything else.

I am also grateful to Toni and Kenneth Brooks and my other friends in Florence, Alabama, who welcome me to speak in their fellowship occasionally, let me talk about Jesus when the Spirit moves me, and who recently said the most amazing words to me: "We want you to be yourself with us." Thank you for making me welcome.

And, finally, while this collection of stories about church ladies of the South is mostly about older women, I am so deeply proud and touched to see my much younger nieces living out their faith and using their gifts as Jesus calls them to. I send my special love to Rhonda Helms, Sarah Helms, Jan Hrivnak and Lola Leigh McCord.

Made in United States
Orlando, FL
12 October 2023

37829166R00095